# Ruthless Games

Ruthless
Book 2

Roxy Sloane

Roxy Sloane Books

Copyright © 2022 by AAHM Inc/Roxy Sloane

All rights reserved.

No part of this book may be reproduced in any form or by any electronic or mechanical means, including information storage and retrieval systems, without written permission from the author, except for the use of brief quotations in a book review.

Cover design by British Empire Designs

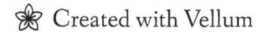

❦ Created with Vellum

# Also by Roxy Sloane

## THE FLAWLESS TRILOGY:
1. Flawless Desire (Caleb & Juliet)
2. Flawless Ruin (Caleb & Juliet)
3. Flawless Prize (Caleb & Juliet)

## THE RUTHLESS TRILOGY:
1. Ruthless Heart (Nero & Lily)
2. Ruthless Games (Nero & Lily)
3. Ruthless Vow (Nero & Lily)

## THE PRICELESS TRILOGY
1. Priceless Kiss (Sebastian & Avery)
2. Priceless Secret (Sebastian & Avery)
3. Priceless Fate (Sebastian & Avery)

## THE TEMPTATION DUET:
1. One Temptation
2. Two Rules

## THE KINGPIN DUET:
1. Kingpin
2. His Queen

Explicit: A Standalone Novel

Also by Roxy Sloane...

## THE SEDUCTION SERIES:

1. The Seduction
2. The Bargain
3. The Invitation
4. The Release
5. The Submission
6. The Secret
7. The Exposé
8. The Reveal

Ruthless : Book Two

Ruthless Games

He was the boy I loved. Now, he's the man who wants me dead.

I struck an impossible bargain to protect the ones I love. I thought I could win his mercy.

But Mafia boss Nero Barretti doesn't know the meaning of the word.

Now, the stakes of this twisted game are higher than ever.

And the passion runs even hotter.

Because it's not just my life on the line anymore.

It's my heart.

THE RUTHLESS TRILOGY:

1. Ruthless Heart

2. Ruthless Games

3. Ruthless Vow

# Nero

I've had this ring waiting for ten goddamn years. A simple gold band. My mother's ring. I kept it in a box at the back of a dresser drawer, waiting patiently for the day I'd earned the right to slide it on Lily's finger.

Where it belonged.

Back then, it was a sign of my love for her. Our trust. A promise of the brighter tomorrow we could share together.

Now, that future is nothing but darkness. But I'll take it from her, all the same.

I'll take everything she has. And more.

This ring will be a testament to her betrayal. Binding her to me, like her web of lies.

I thought I'd love her forever. Now I'll hate her until the day I die.

My prisoner.

My *wife*.

She has no idea, this is just the beginning.

# Chapter 1

## *Lily*

I'm not someone who grew up imagining their perfect wedding day. The girls I knew in school would gossip about it all the time, spinning magical fairytales of the stunning white dress, the music, the flowers. But I never thought much about it. It seemed too far away.

A dream that would present itself to me, in time.

But it turns out, I did have hopes, after all. I assumed my family and friends would be gathered to celebrate us, that I would walk down the aisle full of joy, eager to start my life with my new husband—the man I would love completely. Trust him with my life. Vow with all my heart to honor until the day I died.

It couldn't be further from the truth.

Because here I am, on my wedding day, standing beside the man set to be my husband. But there are no excited friends supporting me, just two nameless thugs here to bear witness in a windowless office. No flowers, or gorgeous white dress, just the plain black shift I was allowed to grab from my closet on the way to City Hall.

And as for my husband, the one I've vowing to join with in holy matrimony?

He's the man who wants me dead.

"Do you swear you enter into this union freely?" The officiant shoots me an anxious look. He can tell that there's nothing normal about the ceremony.

I give a weak nod.

"You, uh, need to say it," he adds, glancing at the man beside me: feared mob boss, Nero Barretti. He could end the registrar with a single word, and the man knows it.

"Yes," I whisper. "It's fine." It's not like I have any other choice. Marry the man who hates me, or die at the end of his gun.

"Can we get on with this?" Nero demands roughly. The official tugs at his collar nervously, and gets back to the vows, reading them so fast, I can barely make them out.

"I do." Nero says curtly, when he's done.

"I do." I echo.

And just like that, it's over. I sign the paperwork they put in front of me and let Nero usher me back out to the car. I slide in the backseat after him, and sit there, numb, watching New York City blocks blur past.

I can't believe it. It's done.

I'm no longer Lily Fordham. I'm Lily Barretti now, permanently connected to one of the biggest criminal organizations on the east coast.

I'm Nero's *wife*.

"I guess we should toast." Nero's voice is full of scorn. He pops the cork on a bottle of champagne, and drinks straight from it before offering it to me with a sneer. "Darling," he says, and the sarcasm in his tone makes me wince.

Celebrate? Ha. There's nothing to celebrate here.

"No thanks."

He shrugs and takes another gulp. "I guess that the honeymoon is over before it even began."

I can't stand his flippant tone—or the wrath that's still seething behind his gaze.

"So, is this how it's going to be?" I demand. "You kept me alive just to torment me with this sham of a forced marriage? I'd rather be dead than have to spend the rest of my life with you!"

Nero's smirk turns to steel. "What did you expect after talking to the FBI?"

"I've told you, I didn't tell them anything!" I protest. "They wanted to cut a deal, make me turn informant against you, but I didn't accept. I would never have betrayed you like that."

"Oh really?" Nero snorts. "You're your father's daughter. Betrayal runs in your blood."

I exhale. There's no escaping the past between us, no matter what I do, it all comes back to that. Ten years ago, I was in love with Nero, when my father cut a deal with the Feds to testify against Roman Barretti. It got him sent to prison and struck a major blow to his empire, and meanwhile we were whisked off into Witness Protection so fast, I didn't have a chance to say goodbye.

I never saw Nero again—until last month, when he found me by accident in my new life. He would have killed me, in retribution for my father's old betrayal, but I managed to negotiate a deal with him, instead: I would help him infiltrate the high society world he needed in order to secure a big real estate deal. The ploy worked: I helped him get close to the politician he needed to make his plans happen, but before the deal was done, the Feds came knocking. They offered me a deal to turn against Nero. And when he found out I'd been talking to them...

I thought for sure I was dead.

But instead, I discovered there's a fate worse than death.

Marriage.

What I don't understand yet is why.

"You think this will keep me from testifying against you?" I ask, trying to figure it out. The shock is fading now, and I'm trying to think ahead. "Some loophole that means if we're married, they can't force me to turn?"

"You always were a smart one." Nero replies bitterly. He gulps more champagne. "It's a little thing called 'spousal privilege'. My lawyers told me about it. They can't compel you to turn against me, due to the sanctity of our bond," he adds, mocking.

I exhale. So, he chose this as a way to keep me under his thumb.

"Why not just kill me?" I ask. "Wouldn't that have saved you the trouble?"

"Now, where would the fun be in that?"

Nero gives me a chilling smile, and I feel a pang. Only days ago, I thought there might be a chance for us. A way for us to be together despite all this mess.

But that was just the lust talking. I couldn't have been more wrong.

I think fast. "What about Teddy?" I ask, panicking at the thought of my younger brother. He's the reason I struck the deal in the first place, to protect him. He's safely off at college right now, oblivious to everything that's been going on.

And I plan to keep it that way.

"What about him?" Nero asks. He didn't bother to wear a suit for our sham of a wedding; he's still in dark jeans and a black T-shirt, with three-day stubble on his jaw.

Dangerous. Sexy as hell.

"You can't go after him."

Nero meets my eyes. "You're in no position to give me orders, *wife*."

I shiver. How many times did I used to imagine that word on his lips? Now, it sounds like a curse.

"Please," the word sticks in my throat, but I force it out. "You have what you want. You won. I'm tied to you now, if you go down, so will I. Spare Teddy, keep him out of this. *Please.*"

"What I want...?" Nero echoes, a strange expression flashing across his face. He grabs my wrist, gripping it painfully. "You think being married to you like this is what I want?!"

I recoil at the anger in his eyes. He loathes me, it's clear.

Being joined in matrimony is just as much a hell for him as it is me.

"Then why?" I demand, frustration rising. "Why put us both through this if you can't stand to be around me?"

"Because I had to," he grinds out. "To protect—"

"The Barretti empire," I finish, scornful. "Of course. It always comes first to you."

Nero wrenches his hand away.

"Stop on Perry Street," he orders his driver, and turns away. The ride passes in silence, until we pull up on a quiet, leafy street in the West Village.

"Get out." He orders me.

I do as he says, looking around. We're parked in front of an elegant brick-faced townhouse. Three stories tall, it has arched windows and a tree bed built into the sidewalk. There's a Dogwood growing there with beautiful white flowers.

"Where are we?" I ask, confused. I assumed I'd be back on lockdown at his loft, a prisoner again.

Nero doesn't answer, he just strides up the front steps and enters a code on the security pad. I follow, looking curiously around. I would never have expected Nero in this part of town: It's all quiet luxury, with tree-lined streets and designer boutiques nearby.

I follow him across the threshold. Inside, it's gorgeous, the foyer tastefully furnished with fine art and modern furniture. The walls are white, and there's tons of natural light coming in through the big windows, opening up to a huge living room, and an open kitchen beyond with warm oak cabinets and a glass wall overlooking the backyard.

A backyard! In Manhattan!

"What is this place?" I ask, looking around and feeling a stab of envy. It's pretty much my dream house, right down to the colorful, elegant furniture in velvets and leather.

"Home."

Nero's reply is curt. I double-take in disbelief.

"What?"

"Welcome home, Princess."

There's nothing welcoming about his voice. "I don't understand..."

"I'm a married man," he replies, still scornful. "Moving up in the world. Why wouldn't I live in luxury with my darling wife?"

"Nero..."

"Your things will be brought. Do what you will."

I glance to the stairs. The bedrooms beyond. He catches my look.

"Which room is mine?" I venture.

"You mean *ours*," he smirks.

"No." I gulp.

"Oh really?" Nero strolls closer. "That's not what you were screaming the other night. *Yes*, you begged me. *Yes. Please. More.*"

I shake my head, tears stinging in my eyes. He's mocking me. Mocking our passion.

"That was before."

"Before you stabbed me in the back."

"Nero," my voice cracks. He turns away, like he's disgusted by my tears.

"Pick whatever room you want. Tell yourself you'll be sleeping alone..." he looks back at me, with a new knowing smirk on his face. "But we both know that's a lie. You'll be at my door soon enough, begging for another dirty screw. Desperate to get that tight pussy throbbing, the way only I can get it wet."

"No." I shake my head, even as my pulse kicks from his filthy words.

He lets out a harsh laugh.

"We'll see about that, Princess. Just try getting off without me. Fucking was all we were ever good for, so why not be honest with yourself? Admit there's still something you want out of this marriage. My cock."

He walks out before I can throw something at him, leaving me alone in the house.

My new house.

I sink down on a chaise and let out a long breath, my emotions in a whirl as I look around the luxurious furniture and serene décor—the opposite of the chaos I'm feeling inside.

In just a few hours, my whole world has changed. Again.

Is this really what I have in store for me now: A lifetime of hostility with Nero?

Nero. *My husband.*

Oh God, what have I done?

## Chapter 2

## *Lily*

My marriage may be a sham, but after a few days, I start to notice that the ring on my finger comes with a few benefits. Nero finally relaxes his tight leash.

The man has been suspicious and tracking my whereabouts as much as possible since I was brought to New York. But it seems that he thinks there isn't much to worry about now that I'm his wife. He has a point. I'm tied to him now, whether I like it or not. Our fates are intertwined.

That doesn't change the fact that he's been ignoring me for days. I've been sleeping in a lavish bedroom down the hall from the primary suite, ignoring him as he comes and goes. And he's repaid me the favor, barely speaking a word to me, even when we pass in the hall. I've still got a driver and full access to Nero's credit cards, so I still can go through the motions of a regular routine. That means lunches with old friends like Marissa, shopping, and even going to the spa.

We're like roommates.

Incredibly twisted, toxic roommates, who still have an inconvenient chemistry between them, threatening to spark to life at every turn.

At least I have my art. This big townhouse has plenty of space, and it only took one quick walk-through of the home to choose a room on the third floor as my new art studio. It's a large, open space near the back of the house with French doors leading to a rooftop terrace. Nero doesn't venture up here, so it's been my sanctuary, and I spend most of my days shut away up here, losing myself in the color and light of my creations, trying to ignore the ugly reality lurking just outside the doors.

But I can't ignore it forever.

"Morning."

I look up in surprise to see Nero in the kitchen as I wander in, barefoot. I'm not much of an early riser, and he's usually gone by the time I leave my room. So seeing him sitting at the table with a toasted bagel in front of him, sipping on a cup of black coffee, immediately puts me on edge.

Something's up.

"What are you doing here?" I ask, pausing in the doorway.

"I live here." He barely glances at me as he speaks, and I sigh.

"You know what I mean."

"Sit down, *honey*," he says, putting a sickly sweet emphasis on that last word.

He's enjoying this.

Instead of obeying immediately, I go to the pantry and grab a box of cereal. I take my time filling a bowl and adding milk, a small act of defiance against my dear husband.

He's patient, which irritates me. I feel like I've lost all the power in this relationship, like I can't get under his skin anymore, but his cold aloofness is driving me crazy.

I lean against the kitchen island and start eating, deciding to wait for him to speak.

"We're going to throw a party, here." he says, and I look over at him in surprise.

"What?"

His signature smirk makes an appearance.

"A celebration of our marriage. Oh, and the real estate deal going through. That's worth celebrating as well. McKenna officially voted yes. The plans are being fast-tracked. There's nothing left in my path."

I exhale. "Congratulations."

He looks at me like I'm being sarcastic, but to my surprise, my words are genuine. "You worked hard enough to make it happen," I give him a careless shrug to cover it. "Kidnapping, blackmail, extortion... I just hope it's worth it."

His lips curl in a smile. "Oh, it will be. I've been getting quotes from real estate guys... Once the land is redeveloped, it'll be worth billions."

*Billions.*

No wonder he'll stop at nothing to be rid of any threat.

"So, a party." I slurp my cereal. "Fine. Whatever."

"You'll need to plan it," he says. "I want no expense spared. I'm making a statement."

"That Nero Barretti is the king of the world?" I quip sarcastically.

He grins. "Sounds good to me. Have everything ready. A week from today."

"No chance," I snort. "That's not enough time. The best caterers are booked months in advance. Event planners, rentals..."

"Make it work." He cuts me off, rising to his feet. "Money talks, and I don't care what it costs. I want the world to see that they can't fucking underestimate me anymore. It's a whole new ballgame. Take care of it."

I scowl at his tone. " "Just because you're my husband, that doesn't mean you're the boss of me.""

Something flashes in Nero's eyes. He prowls forward until he's standing right in front of me. "Interesting," he muses, just looking like he's going to hoist me up on the counter and fuck me senseless.

*Like I want him to.*

"I thought you love it when I tell you what the fuck to do," Nero continues, darkly sexual. "Like when I ordered you to get on your knees and suck my cock. You couldn't get down there fast enough, you were so wet to open wide and take every inch."

Desire locks in my lower belly and spreads like wildfire at the memory. *Fuck.*

He gives a laugh, and it's clear that my body's response is written all over me.

"Yeah, thought so, Princess," his eyes flash with knowing. "Been keeping those fingers busy at night, rubbing that clit raw remembering how good I give it to you?"

"You?" I manage to retort. "No, you're not the one on my mind. In fact, in the list of my past lovers, you barely even rank."

I turn on my heel and stalk out, his laughter echoing after me at my blatant lie.

I'm furious—at myself. I don't want to be turned on by those words. I don't want to think about the way he dominates me in bed and just how good it feels. So, I push my treacherous desires aside and grab on to the nearest distraction full throttle.

If he wants a party, I'll give him a goddamn party.

. . .

For the next few days, I'm the living embodiment of the phrase *shop 'til you drop*.

It strangely gives me some perspective about my situation. Yeah, I'm stuck in a loveless marriage with a man who wants me dead, but I'm still breathing, aren't I? Not just breathing, either, but living in the lap of luxury, doing whatever I want with my time.

And the most important thing is that Teddy is safe. Nero might have blown me off when I pushed him to recommit to our deal, but he hasn't said otherwise, either. I believe that he's going to leave my brother alone. I gave Teddy my real phone number so that we can keep in touch properly. No more sneaking around with burner phones.

It buzzes again as I browse for table settings.

'Study buddies,' the text says, with a picture of his roommates all passed out over their books.

I smile. He's been sending me regular updates and pictures of his life at college in Indiana. He has friends, classes—and no idea what's going on with me.

That's the way I want it. It makes everything worthwhile.

I text back a quick thumbs up.

"Mrs. Barretti?"

It takes me a second to realize the sales associate is talking to me. I'm still not used to the name.

"Yes, hi, sorry." I tuck my phone away.

"The event planner suggested a couple of options, if you'd like to pick."

"Thank you." I follow her to the display. Nero was right, despite being super-last-minute, his cash said all it needed to say. I was able to poach the best event planner in town (courtesy of Marissa's recommendation) and have them put together an incredible party in no time. Now, I'm just confirming a few details for the big event.

## Ruthless Games

"We have plain, or a more deco style," the clerk says, pointing out the options.

"Hmmm..." I couldn't care less about the party but obsessing over the details has distracted me from the chaos that is my life. "Do you have anything in the crystal?"

The woman's eyes light up—probably at the thought of her commission. "I'll go check."

She disappears.

"I like the plain."

A voice beside me makes me startle. I turn.

It's Agent Greggs.

*Fuck.*

I look around quickly. Luckily I'm in the back room of the store, away from the windows, but still... "Were you this careless when you were my father's handler?" I snap, moving behind a shelf of cocktail glasses.

He follows.

"The window is closing for you to make a deal with us," he says. "My boss is gunning for arrests," he continues. "Now that you're a Barretti, she won't hesitate to bring you down too. I've talked her into giving me a little more time to get you to become an informant, but you need to make a decision now. Make the right one."

I fold my arms and glare at him. "Tell me this... Can you guarantee my safety?"

"We'll do everything in our power to—"

"That's not a guarantee." I interrupt. "You lose witnesses all the time. Nero found me in Vegas. Sure, it took ten years, but it happened."

"And if Nero is in prison? Somewhere that he can't get to you? Just consider it," Greggs implores. "Now that the two of you are married... It'll be even harder for you to escape his downfall. You could be tried as an accessory, a coconspirator..."

"But I don't know anything!"

"Is that really true?" Greggs challenges, and I fall silent.

Sure, Nero hasn't told me anything about his business, but that still doesn't mean I haven't witnessed enough incriminating things in our short time together. The beating and likely murder of that rapist, his blackmailing a sitting City Council member...

Which, oh yeah, I was party to.

"I thought so." Agent Greggs sighs, looking at me with real regret in his eyes. "I'm doing what I can for you, Lily, because of your father. But you have to help me."

"I have to plan this party," I correct him, trying to keep my voice light. "And also stay alive. Let me know when you can guarantee either."

"Be smart," he implores me. "You need to protect yourself. Your *new husband* isn't going to do it."

He leaves me be, and I go back to shopping, but I can't get his words out of my head. I know that he's probably just trying to further his own career, to make himself look good in front of his boss by turning me, but that doesn't make his words untrue.

I feel like I'm walking on a tightrope. Nero must still find me useful, especially if he wants to keep up appearances with New York's elite. And by marrying me, he's trying to make it impossible for me to sell him out to the Feds. But for how long will this uneasy truce hold?

When will the scales of value shift, which side will I be left standing on?

*Be smart.*

Agent Greggs is right about that, at least. I need to figure out my own path out of this mess, and I won't find it by filling my days with china place settings and spa treatments.

I need to tell Nero about this little encounter, before

someone else does it for me. It may not earn me his trust, but it'll buy me more time to figure shit out.

So, I finish up at the store, and direct my driver to take me to Nero's office at the club.

Kyle meets my eyes in the rearview mirror. "Is he expecting you?"

"I need to talk to my husband," I say breezily, as if we both don't know what a lie that word is. "About the party."

Kyle starts the engine and moves off, but he places a call through his headset, murmuring low so I can't hear.

It's pretty obvious who he's calling.

When we arrive at the club, I breeze through the bar, faking a confidence I don't really have. I head down the hallway to Nero's office—then stop.

His door is open, and I can see him inside behind the desk. With Avery.

Her head is bent close to his, signing some papers, and he laughs at something she says, looking relaxed. At ease.

I feel an unfamiliar feeling strike, hot in my chest.

*Jealousy.*

I don't know Avery well. She's beautiful, and young, and has a close relationship with him, I know, I just don't know for sure how intimate it is. But as I stand in the hallway, I can't help noticing how easily they interact with each other. They're talking and joking. It's too familiar. There's an ease to this interaction that the two of us never have. Not since we were teenagers.

Avery makes another joke, and Nero rolls his eyes, pushing her playfully.

Before I can think twice, I march straight into the office.

"Lily?" Avery looks up, surprised.

"What are you doing here?" Nero asks, narrowing his eyes.

I don't reply, I just walk right up to his desk, lean over, grab him by the collar and kiss him.

Hard.

Our lips meet, hot and sweet, and the familiar rush washes over me. Fuck. But that's not what I'm here for. I force myself not to fall into his arms, instead, I kiss him slowly and deliberately.

*Marking my territory.*

Then I reel back, stunned. What the fuck did I just do?

Avery clears her throat. "I'll, umm, talk to you later." She shoots a smirk at Nero, and then leaves us alone, closing the door behind her.

"Well, that was a surprise." Nero sounds smug. "Missing me already?"

I clear my throat, flushing. "I need to make myself known as your wife." I say, trying to sound icy. "Just because our marriage is a sham, that doesn't mean you can humiliate me by running around in front of everyone. So, if you're thinking of cheating on me, forget about it."

Nero looks even more satisfied. "Any time you want to come consummate our marriage, Princess, you let me know. But until then..." he trails off.

I glare. "OK. If you want to go cheat with every woman you see, then maybe I'll do the same thing. Find myself a nice side piece to keep my bed warm."

Nero is out of his chair before I've finished speaking.

"You won't do that," he says, rounding the desk to me. He moves so I'm trapped up against it, his hands gripping the wood on either side of me.

My pulse kicks. I try not to shake at his commanding presence.

"Try me," I shoot back.

"Oh, I have..." Nero's predatory gaze skims over my body. I

shiver, and in my thin silk sundress, my nipples go hard. "I've tasted you… Fucked you… Tried every inch of this sweet body. And that's why I know you won't go find another man."

I swallow, tension tightening my core. "Why not?" I whisper.

"Because nobody can give it to you the way I do." Nero reaches out and takes my jaw between his fingers. It's just one touch, but heat suffuses my whole body. He holds my face, forcing me to look at him.

"Nobody fucks you so hard, so damn deep." Nero growls. "They think you're a classy princess? Well, my Princess likes it rough, doesn't she? Pinned to the mattress, moaning, dripping all over my cock."

I shudder, biting back a gasp.

He grins, dangerous. Eyes locked on mine. "I could put you over this desk right now, just shove that dress up around your waist and bury every inch in that sweet candy cunt. Give you the ride you've been waiting for, leave my handprint all over your ass."

His fingers trail down from my jaw, along my throat, over the neckline of my dress. I go weak, fire racing along the path of his touch.

"Would that make you happy, baby?" he asks, teasing over the slope of my breast. "Mark your territory, clawing up my back. We can leave the door open if you want, so everyone can see. Hell, maybe I'll invite Avery back to join us," he adds with a smirk. "No need to be jealous, there's plenty to share. You can ride my face while you tell her exactly how to suck my cock."

I wrench away with a gasp. "You're disgusting," I curse, shaking.

Nero laughs. "Yeah, but you're still too wet to stand."

With that crude parting shot, he walks out, leaving me gasping there with fury—and desire.

I wish I hadn't kissed him like that. I gave myself away and let him know that I feel something for him, despite everything. Possession. Lust. Plain, raw sexual need.

And what's he going to do with that information now?

My blood runs hotter at the thought.

*Damn it.*

## Chapter 3

### *Lily*

Nero isn't a man who likes to waste time. The morning of our big celebration party, it's the ground-breaking ceremony on his new development downtown. A couple of the older buildings have already been razed to the ground, and now a few dozen people are gathered on the construction site to mark the official launch of Barretti Enterprises' jewel of a new construction. There's press, city planners, and all kinds of prominent people milling about.

And me, of course. Nero's loving wife. Dressed in Chanel and a hard hat, and the biggest fake smile I can manage.

"This way, one more shot?"

I turn, and wave for the cameras beside Nero, who looks more and more like a legitimate businessman every day. From his tailored black suit with the gold cufflinks to his winning smile, he fits right in with these people.

But I know the real man behind that mask. The dark mafia king who's made this day happen by breaking every rule in the book.

"Gorgeous, thanks!" the photographer calls.

"Are you talking about me, or my wife," Nero jokes, getting a laugh from the crowd.

My eyes land on a tall figure making his way through the crowd. It's Ian McKenna, and his wife, Fiona, is at his side. I know that my expression falters when I spot them, but I can't help it. It's hard to play the part of dutiful wife when I'm being bombarded with the memories of what happened the last time that I saw the couple. Nero was a monster, cold and calculating as he blackmailed the politician for his vote to rezone this land. Fiona had been there, and I watched her heart break as she saw the pictures Nero presented, showing her husband cheating on her with a younger woman.

There's a slight nudge in my side, and I turn to Nero. His smile is still in place, but there's a warning in his eyes.

My own smile slips back into place as McKenna approaches. "Good to see you, councilman," Nero says loudly, reaching to shake the man's hand.

McKenna grips it, shaking. There's a smile on his lips—but murder in his eyes. He doesn't want to be anywhere near this event, but I'm guessing Nero made it clear that he had to show.

"Wouldn't miss it. I support all development that will enrich this city."

The two of them turn to face the cameras. It's all smiles and handshakes for the crowd while Fiona and I stand at their sides. But I'm close enough to hear the men talk to each other, quiet enough so nobody else hears.

"I hope you're happy," McKenna says. "You've pulled it off, not caring about the cost."

"Who says I don't care?" Nero replies, pleasant. "I'm always willing to spend the money."

"I'm talking about my Fiona. My marriage is crumbling thanks to you."

Nero snorts. "You go ahead and act like I'm the bad

guy here if you want, but we both know that you fucked up and broke the woman's heart. I just decided that you cheating on your wife is something she should know about."

"You enjoyed telling her, you bastard."

"Careful, McKenna." Nero warns, smirking. "You don't want anyone to hear you using foul language. What will the voters think?"

I see McKenna's grip tighten on Nero's hand for a moment. Then they release each other, and McKenna addresses the reporters.

"I'm so glad that you're all here today to record this moment. It's the beginning of something big for this city. Nero Barretti has a vision for this city, and I, for one, am excited to see it come to fruition."

As his little speech comes to an end, he starts to step away. I know that I should just let them go, but I can't seem to help myself as I speak up.

"Fiona, it's nice to see you again."

She looks at me, and the sadness in her eyes shows, just for a moment. "Of course. You too. And congratulations on the wedding."

"Thank you," I reply. I want to tell her that we're both in the same boat, faking affection for the men at our sides, but I know she hates me too. I'm part of her heartbreak and humiliation.

"Come on, Fiona," McKenna says harshly. "We should move along. I'm sure the newlyweds have plenty of people to talk to."

"Speaking of that," I pipe up. "We're hosting a party tonight. A little celebration. We'd love to see you there."

Fiona gives a thin smile. "Sorry, we already have other commitments."

She follows her husband away. He reaches to help her over a pothole, but she doesn't touch him.

"Why did you invite them?" Nero asks.

I shrug. "It seemed the right thing to do."

He shakes his head. "McKenna's old news. He's played his part in all of this already. I don't need him anymore."

I can't help but wonder, what will happen to me when I've played *my* part?

After the ceremony is over, we head back to the townhouse, which is already full of caterers and staff prepping for the party.

"Lily!" my event planner, Beatrice, grabs me on the way in. "I need you. Come..."

She drags me off to approve flowers and appetizers, and I barely have a moment to change before the valet starts showing people in, and the event is underway.

"It really is a spectacular showing, if I say so myself," Beatrice quips, looking around after the guests arrive.

I have to agree. The menu is perfect, a buffet groaning with the finest lobster and caviar, plus an expert mixologist whipping up amazing cocktails at the makeshift bar. The theme is French luxury chic, so there are olive trees, fresh-cut roses, and the smell of lavender is in the air. There's a jazz trio playing in the sitting room, and in the kitchen, a patisserie chef from the finest French restaurant in the city whipping up treats to order.

It's a slice of Paris right here in Manhattan, and it's not lost on me that I've conjured a scene from one of my paintings—trying to feel like anything about this night is genuine or real to me, and not just one big display of Nero's wealth and growing power.

"Not bad." The man himself joins us, and Beatrice tactfully

melts away. Nero looks around the room, every inch the host, surveying his kingdom.

"Not bad?" I echo, annoyed. "I pulled off the impossible here. Nobody expected *this*; you can tell from their faces the moment they walk in."

It's true. The house is filled with society types and business titans, sipping champagne and pretending like they're not paying tribute to a mafia king.

"Fine," Nero agrees with a faint smirk. "I'll admit. I'm impressed."

"Thank you," I say coolly, smoothing down my silk dress.

"Look at this place, it's amazing!"

I turn to see Caleb and Juliet Sterling, making their way through the crowd. I've gotten to know Juliet a little over the past few weeks, and I like her, but not enough to confide the truth about my situation. As far as they know, Nero and I are a real couple, reunited after all this time apart.

"Hi," I greet her, pleased. At least there's one friendly face I know here. "Have you tried the fresh eclairs yet? They're divine."

"Sign us up." Juliet beams. Her husband, Caleb, is more reserved beside her. He has a tangled history with Nero, considering they recently discovered that they're half-brothers.

Caleb nods to him. "I hear congratulations are in order," he says evenly. "You're a lucky man."

"Aren't I just?" Nero replies dryly.

Juliet quickly covers. "I can't believe you just up and did it at City Hall! I would have thrown you a bachelorette," she chides me. "And what about your dress? Who was the designer? I want to see all the photos."

Photos? We didn't take any. They would have only shown the mockery we were making, rushing through the vows, glaring at each other.

I force a laugh. "There's not much to see. I know it was all so quick, but that's how it is sometimes, the heat of the moment. We just share such a deep connection that I didn't want to wait a single day to become his wife."

I hate lying to Juliet like that, but the truth needs to stay between me and Nero.

"I can understand that," Juliet replies, reaching over to take Caleb's hand. They gaze at each other for a moment with love in their eyes, and I try not to feel a pang of regret.

I want to be looked at like that, to feel that way. With my husband.

"Now, how about those pastries?" Juliet slips her arm through mine and steers me away from the guys. "Whatever the... *circumstances* around the wedding," she says tactfully, "You're part of the family now. I'd love for the two of us to get to know each other better."

"Of course," I agree, happy. "I'd love that."

"What do you think about a double date?" Juliet asks.

I freeze—until I see the humor in her eyes. She's kidding.

I laugh, relieved. "Sure, why not?" I joke. "I can just see Nero and Caleb bonding over some bro-time."

"They'll be watching sports together in no time." Juliet smirks, and I laugh again, trying to picture the two brooding, powerful men kicking back over a beer.

Never going to happen.

But it shows that Juliet isn't oblivious to the reality of our situations, which only makes me like her more. Sure, I still have to pretend I'm wildly in love with Nero, but I'd take lying only 50% of the time with her over the 100% it takes to hang out with any of the other people in the room.

"I'll call you," I promise. "We'll hang out soon."

I wish I could stick to her side all night, but I know that Nero would want me mingling. The perfect hostess. And I need to keep being useful, so I leave her with the pastry chef, and circulate, making small talk and connections with the elite guests in attendance.

"I believe you are to thank for this lovely party?"

I pause, turning to the newcomer. He's tall, with dark brown hair, piercing blue eyes, and a European accent I can't place. His designer suit is tailored to fit his slender body, the dark blue color complimenting his pale skin.

I give him a polite smile. "I'll take credit for hiring the party planner, but that's all."

He chuckles. "So modest, too. You must be the new Mrs. Barretti."

"Yes, I'm Lily," I reply, offering him my hand.

Instead of shaking it, he brings it to his lips, placing a kiss on the back. I'm not sure why, but something about the way he holds my eyes as he does this sets off warning bells in my mind. Something is off about this guy. I can't quite put my finger on what it is, but if there's one thing I've learned in Nero's world, it's to trust my instincts.

The man releases his grip. "A pleasure to meet you. I'm Sergei."

"Are you a friend of Nero's?" I ask, trying to place him.

He gives a laugh. "Friend? Alas, no. I'm more of an... *Associate*."

I figure that means he's involved Nero's shady dealings somehow.

"Well, I hope you're enjoying the party," I say brightly.

"I am. And I want to wish you luck in your marriage," he adds. "You know, in my country, there is a tradition that a new bride should break a glass outside, in front of her new home, in order to have a happy marriage."

I smile, just imaging hurling a champagne flute to the ground outside. That would raise some eyebrows. "Is that so?"

Sergei smiles. "They say that all conflicts in the marriage will stay outside of the home, much like the broken glass."

"I've never heard of anything like that," I say, interested. "What country are you from?"

"Serbia," he replies—before I feel a tight grip on my wrist, yanking me back.

It's Nero. With fury in his eyes.

"Don't talk to her," he growls at Sergei. "Don't even look at her."

I'm shocked by the barely contained violence in his tone.

"Nero—" I start, but he speaks over me.

"You're not welcome in this house." He moves to place his body between Sergei and me.

There's tension in every line of his muscles, and his hands are balled into fists at his sides. "Get the hell out."

"But why would I leave?" Sergei doesn't seem phased by Nero. He meets his eyes with a cool smile. "When your lovely wife, Lily, has been so welcoming."

Nero flinches at my name. "Get. Out."

He advances, and I look around, anxious. People are starting to look. "Nero... The guests..."

"She's right," Sergei smirks. "We wouldn't want to make a scene." He makes a show of slowly draining his champagne glass and giving me a nod.

" Congratulations on your good fortune," he says to the both of us. "You'd be wise to treasure it... While you still can."

With that subtle threat, he turns and saunters away.

Nero exhales in a rush, still wound tight with tension.

"What was that?" I ask, reeling.

"What did he say to you?" Nero demands, still gripping me tightly.

"Nothing. Just small talk. Nero, you're hurting me," I protest.

He drops his hand. "Sorry."

I clock his mood. This isn't just Nero being a dick for the sake of it, something serious is going on. "Who was that man?" I ask, feeling a chill.

He just shakes his head.

"Nero—" I ask again, but he just grabs a glass from a passing waiter.

"It's none of your fucking business," he says harshly, and walks out.

Not just out of the room—but out of the whole party, disappearing through the crowd to the door.

I watch him go, shocked. What the hell just happened?

## Chapter 4

## *Lily*

Even with Nero making a swift exit, the party continues. I plaster on a smile, make small talk, and mingle, until at last, by one A.M, everyone has finally left the building.

I'm alone.

Well, me and the rest of the staff for the event, cleaning everything up.

"You really don't have to do this," one of them eyes me curiously. I'm still in my silk cocktail dress and a pair of bright yellow rubber gloves. "We'll take care of everything."

"It's fine," I grit out. "It's my mess to clear up."

Mine, and my darling husband's. I angrily shove trash into another bag, stewing over Nero's disappearing act.

How could he just walk out?

He's the one who wanted a fancy party, and I bust my ass to make it happen. He couldn't even pretend to be a happy newlywed for a couple of hours.

"Mrs. Barretti?" a voice interrupts my silent rant.

I startle. Even after spending hours at a party to celebrate my marriage, it feels strange to be called that. I turn. "That's everything packed up," the caterer says. "Unless you need…?"

What, my husband?

"Thank you." I quickly go grab the envelope I set out earlier, filled with a truly astonishing cash tip. "I really appreciate your work. And your discretion," I add.

She clocks the bills stuffed inside, and her eyes widen. "Of course. Call us anytime. Any time at all."

She bustles out, and the cleanup crew follow, then finally, I'm left alone.

I glance at the clock, as if I didn't check it minutes ago.

Nero is still not back. He's been gone for hours.

And I have no idea where he's gone… Or even if he's planning to come home again.

I sink down on a dining chair, looking around the spotless house that couldn't be less like a home. Sure, we put on a good show tonight, but that's all it was. A performance.

Is this what my life is going to be? I wonder. My *marriage*?

That word makes me let out a small, bitter laugh. After an entire evening of pretending that I'm happily married to a man who can't stand the sight of me, it's a relief to finally let it out.

What the hell am I going to do?

I think about what Agent Greggs told me. *'Be smart.'* He was right. I have to protect myself. Nero has made it clear that the ring on my finger doesn't change anything: I'm still just a pawn in whatever twisted games he wants to play. He's not telling me anything, like why that Sergei guy fired him up, or even who half these people were tonight that he wanted to impress.

I may be his wife, but I'm not his partner.

I pause, wondering where that thought came from. I don't want to be Nero's partner in anything! I want to get as far away from the man as it's safe to do so. I was ready to run, just a week ago, and nothing's changed about that. Not really.

But how can I leave now? Our marriage may be a sham, but it still means something in the eyes of the law.

I go retrieve my phone upstairs and find Marissa's number. She was just here at the party with her husband, but they left early. Packing for a trip to the Caribbean.

I'm expecting her voicemail, but she answers on the first ring.

"Hey," she greets me. "Amazing party, I'm so sorry we slipped away so soon. What did we miss?"

"Nothing much," I lie. *Just a mysterious stand-off between Nero and a menacing man.* "I was just going to leave you a message."

"I got stuck into a new episode of *Selling Santa Barbara*, while I was packing," she confides. "Ryan is already passed out. What's up?"

I pause. "I just need a favor."

"Sure thing. Is this about my facialist? Because I swore I wouldn't reveal her name, but for you babe, I'll do it."

"No," I say. "Actually… I was hoping you could point me in the direction of a good divorce lawyer."

My words are met with shocked silence, so I quickly add: "I care about Nero, but I'm wondering if we weren't kind of hasty in getting married so quickly. I don't know, I guess we got swept up in the excitement of it all. But that's wearing off a bit, and… I want to explore my options."

"Of course!" Marissa says. "Buyer's remorse, it happens to the best of us. Don't tell Ryan I said this," she adds, dropping her voice, "but I've always thought all that 'until death do us part' stuff was way extreme. You never know what can happen."

I exhale in relief. "Thanks for understanding. So, do you

know someone? They need to be good. And discreet. Nero... Well, we're not on the same page."

"Say no more," she insists. "I've got just the guy in mind. He got my friend Mindy out of a very tricky prenup. She wound up taking half his company, and all his yacht!"

"I don't care about the money. I just... Want to explore my options."

"I'll see if he's taking new clients," she promises.

I hear the front door open and shut, and panic.

"I've got to go," I blurt. "Thank you!"

I hang up, exiting my room and storming down the stairs, meeting Nero as he steps into the foyer. He's looking worse for wear, with his shirt rumpled and the scent of cigarette smoke and booze in the air.

"Seriously?" I exclaim, furious. "Where the hell have you been?"

"Out."

He strolls towards the kitchen, and I follow, my blood running hot with all the unanswered questions. I'm tired of being ignored.

"What the fuck are you playing at?" I demand, my voice rising. "You wanted a party, so I threw one, but you couldn't even do me the courtesy of sticking around. I can't believe you left me here to deal with our guests alone after that scene with Sergei. Whoever the hell he is, because, oh yes, you won't tell me that, either. Is there anything I'm allowed to know?" I ask, grandstanding. "You know, since I'm only your *wife*."

"You want to be my wife?" Nero turns. "Because say the word, sugar, and I'll claim what's mine."

I take a step back, my stomach flipping at the sheer power radiating from him. His walls are down. He has zero fucks to give right now, and it's a terrifying and alluring thing, all at once.

I shake my head. "What I don't understand is why did you marry me if you hate me so much?"

"Who said anything about hate?" Nero strides closer to me, his eyes flashing. "I swore to honor you, didn't I? Protect you. Cherish you. 'Til death parts us. And unlike some people, I keep my damn vows. But lying was always in your DNA."

"I'm not my father," I shoot back, frustrated. "That was ten years ago, and it had nothing to do with me!" Nero gives a scornful snort at that, only making me more angry. "I'm sick of rehashing the past and playing your games. Either tell me what you want with me or let me go!"

I turn to leave, but Nero's bitter laugh stops me.

"You're just mad because you're not pulling the strings this time. Well, get over it, Princess. I'm not some starry-eyed teenager anymore, too cunt-struck to see you for the duplicitous bitch you really are."

I whirl around. "What are you talking about?"

"Don't act dumb with me," he says, eyes dark with bitterness. "Let's at least be honest about that. You fucked around with me, knowing all along that your dad was turning on my family. You acted like you loved me, just to go and stab me in the back."

My jaw drops.

He thought I knew about it? All this time, he's believed I was part of my father's informing?

"Nero," I swallow, a sudden lump in my throat. This is what he's been holding onto, I realize. *This* is what's been between us all along. It wasn't just my father's betrayal he's been punishing me for.

It's because he thinks I betrayed him, even worse than I thought.

"You're wrong," I tell him. "I had no idea what my dad was planning."

He shakes his head. "More lies."

"No!"

I close the distance between us, and grab hold of both his hands. "Listen to me, Nero. I had no idea. The night we spent together, I got home, and found them all waiting. My bags were packed. I didn't have a choice," My voice shakes with emotion, remembering my heartache and confusion. I meet his eyes, desperately trying to make him see. Make him believe me.

"I wanted to stay. I wanted to be with you! But they put me in the car, they said I would be dead if I didn't go with them. I was only sixteen, I didn't have a choice! But it was real for me, Nero. Every word. Every kiss. Leaving you behind was the hardest thing I ever had to do. I loved you.."

I stare into his eyes, fervent, and Nero looks back at me. I can see my words sinking in, as he turns them over, deciding whether to believe me.

"It was real for me," I repeat. "I could never have faked a love like that. It was always real."

Something shifts in his expression. Breaking open. A new light shining through.

And then he's reaching for me.

His lips crash against mine, searching, desperate, and I meet them with sheer, passionate relief. Yes! I sink into his arms, greedily kissing him back, exploring his mouth and tongue as I hold on tight.

Nero picks me up, walking me towards the stairs, but I can't wait. Desire washes hotly over me, and I boldly yank open Nero's shirt, sending buttons flying everywhere. He lets out a sound like a growl and breaks our kiss to yank my dress up and over my head, leaving me in panties and a strapless bra.

"Dammit, Lily," he groans, eyes raking over me. "Do you know what you do to me?"

"Show me," I demand, breathless. I press myself against

him, and Nero doesn't wait. His mouth is on my breast in an instant, sucking and lapping until I moan. He carries me blindly up the staircase, pressing me back against the wall on the landing halfway up. I rock against him, desperate to feel his hard length against my core. Nero growls, nipping on one taut nipple as he thrusts, pinning me back, rubbing his erection hard against my clit.

I cry out in pleasure. "Nero," I gasp. "Oh God, please..."

He takes us down to the floor, until I'm laying spread on the landing, my head propped against the stair riser as he dips his head to my chest again, his tongue lavishing my breasts, one at a time. I close my eyes in bliss, my hands going to the back of his head as he suckles harder, almost to the point of pain.

But that's how it is with him, straddling the thin line between pain and pleasure until I can't take anymore.

"Please," I beg, writhing in his arms. I don't even know what I'm begging for. Just more of him.

All of him.

His hands find my panties, and he rips them off me, the explicit sound filling the empty house. *Oh my God.* "I'll buy you new ones," he groans, already sucking on the inside of my thigh. "Fuck, Princess, I'll buy you the goddamn world if I get to taste this pussy."

I arch up, eagerly pressing myself closer to his mouth. "Yes. Yes!"

I can barely breath as he grips my thighs and spreads my legs wide. He gazes at me, licking his lips.

"You're so wet for me. Fucking *glistening.*"

I shudder with longing. "It's all for you," I gasp. "Please, Nero..."

"I've got you, baby." He growls, his eyes full of lusty victory. "I won't let this sugar go to waste. Not when I've been dying for another taste."

He buries his face between my legs, flattening his tongue as he licks up my center.

I scream.

Holy fuck! My legs shake, and he throws them over his shoulders, keeping me wide open for his tongue as he presses a hand to my stomach, pinning me in place.

Pleasure slams through me, circling tighter with every wicked lick. "Oh my God!" I cry, grabbing hold of the banister spokes with one hand, "Yes!"

"Scream my name," Nero demands. "Tell everyone who's giving it to you so good."

"Nero!" my voice echoes, frenzied with passion. "Oh God, Nero, yes!"

"That's right. Louder."

He devours me again, exploring my folds with swift, probing strokes, wrapping his lips around my swollen clit and suckling there until I scream again. Dear Lord, I'm in heaven, lost under the onslaught of pleasure.

And then he thrusts two thick fingers inside me as he laps relentlessly at my clit, and I just about lose my mind.

"Fuck!"

I climax with a scream. My orgasm barrels through me, and I roll my hips, grinding into his fingers while I ride out the waves of bliss.

But just as quickly, Nero pulls away. "I said I'd claim you, and I meant it." He looms over me, stripping off what's left of his shirt and unbuckling his pants. "This pussy is mine, Princess. My wife's going to take her husband's cock all the way to the fucking hilt," he vows. "You're going to feel me for days, I'm going to fuck you up so good. Because I know, you wouldn't want it any other way."

*Oh my god.*

I shudder, just watching him, so powerful. *All mine.* His

erection is thick and heavy, and I need it like I've never needed anything in my life.

I lay back and spread my legs wider. An invitation.

Nero groans, fisting his fat cock in one hand. "No, baby. Get on your hands and knees for me. I've got to get it all the way deep."

I'm moving before he's finished the sentence, scrabbling to give him what he needs. He sinks to his knees behind me and grips my hips, landing a sharp smack on my ass before he's leaning over, covering me. Trapping me in place.

"You know why animals fuck this way?" Nero demands, breath hot in my ear. I shudder in the warm cage of his body, eagerly bucking back against his cock.

"Why?" I gasp.

"Because it goes so fucking deep."

He drives into me in one hot stroke, sending me slamming forwards, crying out at the glorious intrusion. His thick girth, stretching me wider. Opening me up.

"You feel that, baby?" Nero slams home again, his grip on my hips pulling me back onto his cock.

"Yes!" I cry, because fuck, he's right. He's so deep, I'm seeing stars. Sobbing, writhing, grinding back on his magnificent cock. "Fuck, yes!"

"You belong to me," he grunts, withdrawing, then thrusting deep. Deeper. *Fuck.* "Every inch, every part of you. *Mine.*"

"Yours," I sob, shuddering. My God, I had no idea it could feel this amazing. "I've always been yours."

My halting admission seems to unleash something in him, because he lets out a roar. His pace turns frenzied, rutting into me like a wild animal, rough and dirty and so, so good.

"Yes!" I scream. "Right there, don't stop!"

"Never," he groans, reaching to rub my clit in an explosion

of pleasure. "Fuck, you take it so good. Gonna make my wife come all over this beast of a cock."

I shudder, loving how that sounds. Because in this moment, fuck, I belong to him. It's like he's laying a claim on me. He's showing me who I belong to, marking me as his with the way he dominates my body.

And I let him.

Hell, I want it.

I rock back into him with every forceful push of his hips forward, and I start to feel that electric energy building up in my body again, the kind that can only mean a climax is coming.

"My husband," I chant, thrusting back, grinding. "My husband always gets me there. My husband knows exactly what I need."

"Fuck, Lily, fuck!"

Nero reaches out and grabs my hair, wrapping it around his hand. The bite of pain makes my pleasure soar, and I feel his body tense, to breaking point. "Baby—" he lets out a strangled howl, pistoning into me again as his fingers rubs me, just right.

*Oh my god!*

I climax with a scream, pleasure slamming through me, ripping me apart. Nero drags me up, flush against his body, driving up into me and grinding there as I clench around him. Spasming my orgasm all over his cock.

"Fuck. Baby. *Fuck!*"

He comes with a roar, spurting up inside me, still thrusting, fucking us through the first waves of pleasure—and into the next. Over and over, he pounds into me, until we collapse on the staircase, totally spent.

I gasp for air, stunned. Not just by the sheer force of my pleasure, but by the connection, too.

The way it felt to finally admit I was his.

Nero pulls me into his sweaty arms, breathing fast. He groans, and I laugh.

"Right back at you," I say, exhausted. He spoons me, wrapping his arms tight and dropping a kiss on the back of my neck.

"Guess we finally christened the new house," he says, and I can hear the satisfaction in his voice.

*Our house.* I smile, looking at where our hands are intertwined. There's a simple gold band on both our wedding fingers, and for the first time, I look at it, and feel…

Safe.

Satisfied.

*His.*

I suck in another breath, emotions rushing in, more than just pleasure. I've spent our first week of marriage full of anger and resentment, viewing it as another obstacle to my freedom. But now the words come back to me. We took a vow, *for better or worse.*

But which one are we now?

# Chapter 5
## *Nero*

I don't sleep.

Lily spends the night with me. Lying in bed beside me, sprawled on the bedsheets, asleep to the world. I watch her breathe, trying to imprint this memory, every fucking detail of her perfect face, to store them away in my mind forever.

Who knows how long this peace will last?

As dawn breaks, I leave her sleeping, and head into my office. I shower there, and scrounge up a clean shirt, but despite the fact I'm tired, hungover, and in dire need of breakfast, I can't keep the smile off my damn face.

*She's mine.*

Not just because of a signature on the marriage certificate, or because I've trapped her into an impossible bargain. She said it herself, last night, her cries of pleasure like a drug to my system.

She's mine. She's always been mine.

All these years, I was certain she betrayed me. Roman swore it, everybody said. There was no way she hadn't known, she'd been in on it with her father, keeping me panting after her while they set up the ultimate deal to narc.

And I believed it, too. Heartsick, furious, full of self-loathing. I thought she'd played me for a fool. That betrayal has driven me on, hardened my heart, pushed me down this path of vengeance to become the man I am today. Feared. Revered. *Alone.*

But I was wrong about her. I could see it in her eyes when she made her sobbed confession last night. What we shared was real. She loved me.

*Which means she could, again.*

I shake my head, still trying to get my mind around it. Everything's changed. *Everything.* It's like I woke up this morning and gravity has shifted. This core belief I've built my life on isn't just wrong, but the total opposite. Down is up. Left is right. And Lily...

Lily is my wife.

Not just on paper, but in every way that counts. In my bed. In my arms. Clenching around my cock like a goddamn vice.

Regret slams through me, thinking of the past few weeks of rage and resentment. Hell, the past ten years. If I hadn't wasted all this time hating her...

But the past is dead and buried now. All that matters is what I do now that I know the truth.

Besides getting myself some food.

"Freddie?" I yell. One of the new kids comes running. He's barely seventeen, and his older brother's one of my lieutenants. He tested out of high school early, a smart kid, he'd be wasted on the streets, so I'm thinking about sending him to college, training him up as a lawyer or accountant to keep an eye on our books.

"Yes, boss?"

"Go to Gino's and grab me one of their Godmother subs.

## Ruthless Games

Wait, make it two," I say. "And get something for yourself," I add, tossing him a hundred-dollar bill.

He races off eagerly, passing Chase on the way in.

"Tell me you have coffee," I say, grabbing a bottle of aspirin from my desk drawer and gulping a couple back with a slug of whiskey. I wince. "I'd give you everything in my wallet right now for a decent espresso."

"What the fuck's going on with you?" Chase's expression is pissed. "I've been calling you all night."

I already don't like his tone, but I'm in a good enough mood to let it slide.

"I slept in," I say, passing him in the doorway and heading to our shitty kitchen. The coffee pot's been brewing there for God knows how long, but fuck, it'll do for now. I look around. "When did this place start falling apart? Maybe I should ask Lily to give this place a revamp—or hire someone who will."

There's a beat of silence as Chase stares at me like he's looking at a stranger.

"You want to *redecorate*? What the fuck, man?"

He's right. I shake it off, striding back to my office. "Don't get your panties in a twist," I say, gulping down the sludge that passes for coffee around here. "We don't have to live like animals, is all I'm saying."

"I knew that fancy new place in the Village would go to your head." Chase scowls. "In case you forgot, this is our territory. And the Kovaks are making moves to muscle in."

I tense, remembering Sergei's appearance at the party last night. His hand on Lily.

His warning.

"What have they done?" I demand, moving back behind my desk. All business again. The Kovaks are one of our main rival organizations, out of Serbia with Russian ties. They're a nasty piece of work, alright. Made their money trafficking girls over to work the sex clubs, now they're eying expansion into drugs and guns.

And our turf.

"The usual bullshit," Chase replies, darkening. "Picking fights with our guys, moving product on streets they shouldn't. We can't stand for it; we need to do something. Show them who the fuck they're dealing with."

Typical Chase: Shoot first, ask questions later. He's so focused on the old rules, he can't see the bigger picture.

But I do.

"You need to chill," I instruct him. "I mean it. No moves, no retaliation. The last thing we need is violent gang war fucking up this real estate development. We just broke ground."

Chase slams a fist on the desk. "Fuck the development! Christ, Nero, what the fuck is wrong with you? I'm telling you we've got a serious threat brewing, and all you think about is that damn land. You know what's more important than that? The Barretti name. Our people. We need to make a statement, show those Serbian bastards they can't pull this shit."

I glare.

"You're forgetting who the fuck's in charge here." I say, my voice harsh. Chase has been pushing against me more lately, and I'm losing patience. I know he doesn't approve of the direction I'm taking this empire, but I'm damn sure he'll fall in line.

They all will.

"Look, I'm just saying—"

"I'm the one with Barretti on my fucking birth certificate, so I make the decisions around here," I cut him off, staring him down. Chase exhales, then nods.

"Fine."

"And tell the guys to dial things back at the docks," I add. "We need to keep our hands clean for the time being."

"But what about the Kovaks?"

"They're trying to stir shit. Provoke us into lashing out. I'm not falling for that game."

Chase scowls. But he doesn't argue any more.

"Interesting choice," a voice says from the doorway. I look past Chase to see a tank of a man standing there. He has a shaved head, and full sleeves of tattoos on each arm, and there's something familiar about his weathered face. "What are you planning to do," he continues, "sit back on your ass and let the Kovaks take our territory, one block at a time?"

I frown, trying to place him.

"You better have a fucking good reason to be standing there, talking like that," Chase says, backing me up like a pro.

"Name's Vance." The man drawls, ignoring him. "Roman sent me to help you out."

That's how I know him. I recognize him back from when I was a kid. One of my father's most loyal lieutenants, he got busted with a boat full of product arriving straight from Colombia. They leaned on him hard, but he took a twenty-year sentence and never said a word. He's a legend around these parts.

And now he's a free man, and my problem.

"Thanks for the offer, but I have all the help I need," I say, nodding in Chase's direction. He might be pissing me off lately, but at least I have no doubt that his loyalty lies with me.

"Your father thinks otherwise." Vance's gaze is cold. "Says you could use some... trusted advice, these days."

I bristle. Fuck if I'm going to have someone keeping tabs on me, after everything. But still, I keep it cool. If he's my father's man, there's no use reasoning with him.

Only one man can do that.

"Hey, you know old warriors are always welcome around here," I say, spreading my arms. "Why don't you have a drink at the bar? We've got a twenty-year scotch you won't have tasted in a while. When did you get out, anyway?"

"A couple of months ago. Good behavior." Vance looks more relaxed now.

I chuckle. "Glad to hear it. I'm sure you'll be a great addition to the team. Chase? Take care of our new friend. I've got some business to attend to."

I shoot him a warning look, and he takes the hint.

"Let me hook you up," he says, steering Vance out. "You need anything else? Cash? Pussy? Just say the word."

The minute they're out the door, my smile drops.

Fuck.

There's no way I can stand for this. I've kept my real estate plans under wraps from my father, knowing exactly what he'll think about my aims to take the Barretti empire legit. Over his dead body. He wouldn't care we stand to make millions—if not billions—by moving away from criminal enterprise to the legal side of shit.

He built this empire on blood, and that's all that matters to him.

I've been waiting until things are too far gone to take back, so there's enough money floating around to buy me some loyalty from the rank-and-file. But if Vance is here, keeping tabs on me...

I need to be careful. Play it smart. I'm on the edge of something big here, and nothing can fuck up my plans.

Freddie knocks, then enters, back with my food. "Thanks, kid," I tell him, taking the bag. I pause, getting an idea. "Listen, I've got a job for you. You see the guy with Chase in the bar?"

"Vance Fortinelli?" Freddie asks, wide-eyed. "I've heard about him. My brother says he's old-school."

"I need you to stay close," I tell him. "Keep an eye out,

watch where he goes, and who he's getting friendly with. You can do that?"

He nods. "Sure."

"Good. Keep me updated. And keep this between us," I add.

I need to know everything that's happening under my roof. With so much on the line, I don't need any surprises—from the Kovaks, or Roman.

This is my empire now, and I intend on keeping it that way.

I spent the rest of the day making sure every other part of this business is running like clockwork. I can't afford any mistakes, so I check in with all my deputies, review the books, and meet with Miles to discuss the minor charges a couple of our guys are facing. By the time I'm done, I'm worn out, but as I head back to the townhouse, I find myself getting a second wind. Impatient to see her again.

My wife.

The words still feel foreign, even in my own mind. I let myself in, glad I had them fit state-of-the-art security in every inch of this place. Sergei strolled right in, but it sure as hell won't happen again.

I pause in the foyer. "Lily?" I call.

There's no reply, but I hear music drifting from upstairs.

I head straight for the art studio on the third floor. That's exactly where she is, perched on a stool in front of her easel. I study her profile from the doorway, watching as she nibbles on her lower lip, all of her concentration on the canvas as she layers paint, lost in the music.

She's so goddamn beautiful, it takes my breath away. Strong. Brave. Perfect.

And when I see the gold band on her finger glinting in the

sunset light... I feel a new kind of possession, stronger than anything I've felt in my life before. Whatever Chase or my old man thinks about this marriage, it doesn't matter. Nothing else matters now.

Lily will always be mine.

I don't care what it takes. I'm going to keep her safe and protected, right here with me. I want to come home at night to this very sight, wake up with her every morning. Fuck, I want to see her belly swell with my baby, create a new life for the both of us and make up for lost time.

But can I trust her? I don't even fucking care anymore. I'll protect her, no matter what.

Because I know, I'm the one putting her in danger now.

I feel a chill. Sergei, my father, the Feds... Just having her under this roof has put a target on her back, and now that she's my wife, I know, it won't stop.

Not until I make them stop.

I force myself to turn and walk away, leaving her to paint in peace. As much as I want her, I can't think straight when I'm touching her, and I need my wits about me more than ever. I'm not just fighting for the future of the Barretti organization anymore. I'm fighting for *our* future.

And it's not a fight I'll ever lose.

# Chapter 6

## *Lily*

After that night with Nero, I think we've broken through to a new place in our relationship. And maybe I'm right. There's a new understanding in his gaze when he looks at me, his voice warmer. He even laughs and makes the occasional joke when we cross paths over breakfast or late at night.

But he's still keeping me at arm's length. It's been days since he fucked me to heaven and back, but he hasn't touched me since. He's gone at the office all day, and half the night too, leaving me alone in my bed, aching for him. I should be glad he's giving me space, but I feel like I'm losing my mind with each passing minute, half-ready to just leap on him the moment he walks through the door.

But something makes me hold back. We have an uneasy peace between us, and I don't want to mess it up.

Whatever he's dealing with, I need to handle this right. Because if I throw myself headfirst into this passionate connection, it'll be game over. Good sense out the window. And I need to figure my own emotions out, too.

Like what *I* want from him. What my future holds, in all this madness.

But still, I want him bad.

"Sugar?"

"I thought I was 'baby'," I tease, over breakfast in the sundrenched kitchen. Nero grins, pouring sugar into my coffee.

"You can have both. Greedy girl."

Our eyes lock, and my breath hitches, but before I can flirt some more, Nero turns back to his phone.

Dammit.

I watch him, scrolling on his phone, glancing at the newspaper. He's a million miles away, caught up in work, but all I can think about is him bending me over the kitchen island and screwing me senseless.

My skin flushes hotter. I'm wearing a skirt today, a knee-length, floral thing, so all he'd have to do is hike it up to have full access to me. *Hands reaching... Fingers grazing...* I clench tightly at the thought. I can feel wetness gathering between my thighs.

*What would he say if I showed him?*

I blush hotter at the dirty thought. I should be glad he's being so respectful, not assuming that just because we fucked on the staircase like a pair of animals, I was his to take at will. And yet...

I am. I want to be. And meanwhile, he's completely oblivious.

My phone dings on the table, and I blink, realizing that I've been staring at the island, picturing the scene in my mind.

"Distracted, much?" Nero asks, looking amused.

"Just... Thinking about the painting I'm working on," I lie, grabbing my phone from my bag.

It's a message from the lawyer Marissa put me in touch with. He wants to meet.

Fuck.

I freeze, guilt crashing through me. Thinking about divorce when only moments ago I was imagining Nero buried in me all the way to the hilt?

It feels like some kind of betrayal. But I force myself to stay calm.

"Marissa wants to have lunch and a spa session," I lie.

"Sounds fun," Nero doesn't look up, and slowly, my breathing returns to normal.

I text back, confirming our meeting—and then delete the messages.

"I better go get ready," I exclaim brightly. "Have a great day."

I get up, and I see something flash in Nero's eyes as he looks over me. Something like desire. But he just takes another bite of toast. "You too," he says.

I exit the room, my pulse racing. Sneaking off to meet this lawyer is playing with fire, but I'm trying to be smart.

One night with Nero can't fix all my problems. Even if we're in some kind of truce, everything fucked up about my situation is still here. The Feds are circling, and meanwhile, the ring on my finger binds me to Nero's crimes.

I need some objective advice.


When I arrive at the lawyer's office, I'm greeted by a perky receptionist. She picks up her phone to tell the lawyer I've arrived while I head for a chair in the waiting area, but the door to the lawyer's office opens before I'm even halfway there.

"Mrs. Barretti, please come right in."

This is the first time I've met Mr. Heely in person, and he's older than I imagined, probably in his sixties. Short with silver hair and a kind smile, he's dressed in an expensive suit and as I go into his office, I can see that he does well for himself. It shows in the priceless artwork on the walls and the leather-bound first editions on the wall.

"Marissa says you're the best," I say in greeting, and he chuckles, friendly.

"High praise, I'm sure. I whipped her pre-nup into shape," he says with a wink. "Ryan better not think about cheating, is all I'm going to say."

I smile, relaxing a little. He shows me to the couch and takes a seat opposite.

"So... about this divorce of yours..."

"I'm just exploring my options," I say quickly.

"Always wise," he agrees. "Especially in your position, based on the information you sent."

He says it so delicately, I sigh. "You can be blunt," I tell him directly. "If anyone's going to give it to me straight, I need that from you."

"Very well." He nods, and I can tell by the serious look in his eyes that this isn't going to be a smooth, easy process. "Your options are, I'm afraid, limited."

"What do you mean?"

He gives a wry smile. "Let's start with this mess involving the FBI. It's a tricky situation now that you're married to Nero. The good news is that they can't punish you for not testifying against your husband if they arrest him and find something to charge him with. No obstruction of justice or impeding an investigation...Nothing like that. Spousal privilege protects you —and Nero, too."

"That's what I thought."

"*But* it's a double-edged sword," he says, before I can feel too relieved. "There's a chance that they can include you as a coconspirator, depending on what they charge him with."

I gulp. Agent Greggs warned me about this. "And if I divorced him... That would protect me?"

Mr. Heely nods. "Your best bet is to separate yourself from him completely to protect your future. They can't arrest you *or* make you become an informant if you're not connected to him anymore. The wedding was so recent, I would suggest an annulment. If you can prove you married under duress, and haven't consummated the marriage..."

I blush. "That... Won't be possible."

Andy must see my cheeks turning pink because he clears his throat, straightening papers to avoid eye contact.

"Alright. That's not an option then. We'll have to go with divorce. That's trickier. New York state requires a separation, to prove the breakdown of the marriage before you file."

"Separation?" My heart sinks. "For how long?"

"At least six months. So, I would advise you to move out as soon as possible, and start establishing your independent residence."

I shake my head. "That's not possible. Not right now."

Nero will never let me just live separately like that. And if he knows I'm thinking of leaving him...

Our tenuous peace will be blown apart.

"I'm sorry it's not better news," Mr Heely says.

"No," I say, regretful. "At least I know where I stand now. I'll have to think about all this."

"How about I start preparing the filing?" he suggests. "So it's ready to go, should you need it."

I nod. "Thank you," I say, but the words are hollow.

I feel numb as I leave the office. *Six more months with Nero?*

That feels impossible—and not because I can't stand to be around him.

It's the opposite.

He's already making me fall back in love with him, despite myself. I can't stop it from happening, and I know that it's only a matter of time before he doesn't just claim my body, but my heart, too.

And if he does…Could I bring myself to walk away?

My phone buzzes with a new message as I leave the building. It's Nero. I glance around out of instinct. Has he been watching?

But no. That chapter of animosity is over.

I read the message.

*Meet me at Amelia's at six.*

Amelia's is a swanky restaurant, one of the hottest spots around according to gossip at the party. Another fancy event, I'm sure. And I'll be needed to play the perfect wife.

I sigh. Just another reminder that there's always an ulterior motive with Nero. It's hard to tell where the performance ends and our real feelings begin. Even though we're not trying to get close to the McKennas anymore, Nero's ambitions know no limits.

So what's his new game now?

I dress carefully for the evening, expecting to be on display. I take a long shower, and blow dry my hair into loose waves, then select a navy blue silk dress with a scoop neck, and fabric gathering at my hips. I pause over my lingerie, before picking out a sexy matching set in black lace. These won't be on display to anyone except Nero.

Will he finally make another move?

Or, will I?

I gulp. The sexual tension has been building between us for days, and I know how explosively delicious it would be to

## Ruthless Games

finally give in to the passion. Maybe it's crazy of me to be thinking about him sliding, thick and hard between my thighs, while a part of me is still considering the divorce lawyer's advice, but that's par for the course with Nero.

A part of me will always want him, while another part still looks for a way to escape this confusing mess we're in.

Push and pull. Love and hate. The line blurs a dozen times over, every single day.

Is it any wonder it's so intoxicating?

When I arrive at the restaurant, I'm surprised to see that Nero is waiting out front. He's dressed to impress too, in a dark suit with his hair slicked back. Clean-shaven, piercing eyes...

I feel a shiver of lust as he meets the car and opens my door.

"Hi," I greet him shyly, as his gaze drinks me in. I feel a stab of pride that I picked the right outfit. Right enough to bring that possessive gleam to his expression, anyway. "So, what's the deal tonight?" I ask, as he leads me to the restaurant.

"The deal?"

"Who are we impressing, and why?"

Nero holds the door open, and I follow him inside. Then I pause. I was expecting a big private event, but instead, the restaurant looks normal: couples and groups dining at lavish tables, and a hostess meeting us right away.

"Mr Barretti, I have your table," she says, and leads us through the dining room to a table in the back.

It's a table for two.

I look around, confused. "I thought this was another event," I admit. "You know, more people to charm-slash-impress."

Nero gives me a distracted smile, then turns back to the hostess. "This won't work," he says firmly.

"Excuse me?"

"This table. I asked for the best. This isn't it."

"Nero," I interrupt, "It's fine."

"It's not fine." As if to demonstrate his point, the kitchen doors fly open and a server emerges—just a few feet away from my chair.

The hostess looks troubled. "We're fully booked tonight."

Nero doesn't blink. "I'm sure you'll be able to accommodate us."

"But—"

Before she can object again, a man in a suit comes rushing over. "Mr. Barretti!" he gushes, looking anxious. "Is there a problem?"

"Not if you find a better table for me and my wife."

Nero's still casual, but everything about his body language screams power. Commanding the room without a single harsh word.

I shiver. Is it terrible that I find him so sexy right now?

"Of course, of course," the manager stumbles. "I'm so sorry for the mix-up, please, give me just a moment."

He makes a beeline for the middle of the room: the best table in the house. There's a trio of diners there in the middle of their meal, but all it takes is a word, and they're suddenly being moved to another table. Busboys swoop, servers clear, and in no time at all, we're being settled in our new dining spot.

That's the kind of power that Nero wields so effortlessly. Everybody in this building knows, he's king.

I gulp, cheeks heating as I accept the menu. "Thanks," I mutter.

"Champagne, please, as a personal apology." The manager pours it himself, then melts away.

Nero raises his glass and gives me a smile. "Now, this is more like it, don't you think?"

"I can't believe you just did that." I glance around. People are turning back to their meals, but still, I see the occasional wide-eyed stare.

"Why not?" he gives a shrug. "You deserve only the best."

I roll my eyes, but he's not kidding. I look around again, clocking the candlelight and romantic flowers. And Nero, sitting across the table from me, looking like he wants to devour me right here and now.

My pulse kicks.

"So... Is this a date?" I venture.

"It's dinner," he replies, shaking out his napkin. "With my wife."

I shiver again, I can't help it. Hearing him say the word like that, so confident and possessive... It makes my nipples tighten.

And I can tell, he sees.

"I like that dress," he says, lips curling in a knowing smirk.

I flush, but I try to stay cool. "Tell me the real reason we're here," I try again. "You never do anything without an agenda."

Nero's smile doesn't dim. "I'd say seeing you sitting there, in that dress, is reason enough." His eyes travel over me, hot and blatant, and it feels like he's already undressing me.

My blood runs hotter.

He beckons the waiter over, and orders for us both. When he's gone, I give him a look.

"What if I'd like something different?"

"You like it when I take care of you." He reaches out and takes my hand, rubbing his thumb seductively over my sensitive palm.

*Dammit.* He knows me too well.

"Still..." I say, flirty now. "What if I wanted lobster instead?"

"Then I'll pick up my phone, buy a damn lobster boat, and

have a crate sitting on ice by the time we get home." Nero doesn't break the stare. "When are you going to learn? I get what I want. And right now, I want my wife happy, fed, and screaming my name."

I raise an eyebrow, smirking. "I'm not sure how everybody else here would feel about that last one."

"Fuck them," Nero says boldly. "I would spread you right here on the table, hike up that dress, and make a mess of your pretty cunt in front of everyone. Say the word, baby. To hell with the rest of them."

Heat rushes through me. I see it in his eyes, he means it. He'll do anything he wants...

And what he wants right now is to please me.

A new wave of desire rolls through my core. Fuck, I shouldn't be turned on by his arrogance, but damn if it doesn't get me hot, knowing that this powerful, dangerous man is ready to serve my every desire.

To give me pleasure, no matter what everyone thinks.

"Dessert can wait," I tell him, smiling. "Let's get through dinner first."

He chuckles. "Promises, promises."

Our first course arrives, and of course, it's delicious. "How was your day?" I ask, feeling weirdly self-conscious now that I know this evening is a date.

A romantic one, too.

Nero shrugs. "The usual bullshit. How about you?"

My guilt rears its head again. "Nothing special."

"You saw Marissa, right?"

My eyes dart up. Is he trying to trap me in a lie? "No, actually," I reply, playing it safe. "She couldn't make it. Last-minute thing. So, I walked around a little, stopped by some galleries." I take another bite, and thankfully, he lets the subject drop.

I focus on the food, until I realize, Nero has fallen silent. I look up.

"When you said I always have a reason..." Nero pauses, and I tense, bracing myself for the worst. "I guess you're right. I wanted it to be special when I gave you this."

He reaches into the inner pocket of his suit and pulls out a small, black velvet box.

My heart stops as he places it on the table between us and opens it, revealing a stunning diamond ring from Sterling Cross.

I gasp. Is he serious right now?

"I know it's a little too late for an engagement ring," Nero begins, looking serious. "This isn't how you pictured any of it. The wedding, the way it all went down. It isn't what you wanted. What you deserve. So, I wanted you to have this."

He lifts the ring from the box, and takes my hand, sliding it onto my ring finger next to my wedding band.

"It's so beautiful," I breathe, stunned. The diamond is massive, cut in the princess style, surrounded by smaller, pavé stones.

"Juliet helped me pick it out," he admits, with a wry grin. "I must have looked at every damn ring Sterling Cross had in the building. But I wanted it to be perfect."

My emotions feel out of control as I stare at it, glittering on my hand, knowing he took the time to select something I would like.

"But, why?" I ask, head spinning. I search his face, looking for a clue. *What does this mean?*

"It means, regardless of how we got here, you're my wife now." Nero meets my gaze. "And those vows we took? I'm going to abide by them. And I hope you will, too."

Love. Honor. Obey.

The weight of those words—and this ring—hits me all at once.
*They're real to him.*
*This* is real. Beneath all the lies, and vengeance, and half-truths. Behind the fighting, and desperate passion, we somehow crossed a line to something true.
The bond between us never died. And now he's offering me a chance to love him all over again.
*Forever.*
"I... I..." I stammer, overwhelmed. "I... Will be right back."
I bolt from my chair, fleeing straight for the bathroom. If I sit there for another second, I'm afraid I'll get lost in his eyes forever and start saying things I regret.
I can't do that, no matter how tempting.
Inside the tiled refuge of the restroom, I go straight for the sink, bracing myself with my palms flat on the porcelain. Looking in the mirror, I stare into my own eyes, and I can see the panic there. Nero is saying all the right things, but I already have one foot out the door. I just met with a lawyer *today*.
But I can't lie to myself. I want to be with him. I want him to want me.
I just don't know if I can trust this sudden sincerity.
I feel like my heart and my mind are at war, and it's tearing me apart. The worst thing is that I just want to go back out there and tell Nero that I'm crazy about him. It could be so perfect.
Or he could break my heart into a million pieces.
I run the cold faucet and let the water flow over my wrists, trying to collect myself. I close my eyes and contemplate what I'll say when I get back to the table.
What can I say?
*'I want to love you again, I think my heart already does, but there's so much history, I don't know how we could ever trust*

*each other—and, oh yeah, your criminal empire could come crumbling down at any moment, leaving the both of us in jail.'?*

It doesn't exactly roll off the tongue.

I'm so lost in thought that I barely even glance over when I hear the door of the bathroom open behind me. I register a tall, dark-haired woman, dressed in a skintight dress. She moves towards the sink, so I step aside, assuming she's here to touch up her makeup.

Instead, she grips my arm, grabs a handful of my hair, and smashes my face forwards into the mirror.

Pain bursts along my cheekbone where it makes impact with the glass, and I let out a strangled scream of pain. *What the fuck?* Struggling to recover, I try to pull away, but she's too strong and she has too much leverage in this position, her forearm pressing into the center of my back as she leans close.

"Careful, Mrs. Barretti," the woman says, in a thick Russian accent. "You could hurt yourself like this."

"What... What do you want?" I ask, my throat closing up in fear.

"Consider this a friendly warning." She twists my arm tighter, and I yelp in pain. "Your husband's power is slipping. Who knows what *accidents* you may face next?"

Suddenly, the door swings open, and another patron walks in. "What on earth...?" she blurts in surprise.

The woman releases me so quickly, I stumble, and then she's gone, disappearing out the room and down the hallway towards the kitchens.

"My word," my rescuer gasps. "Honey, are you OK?"

I collapse back against the wall, trying to catch my breath. "I... I don't know."

My fingers come up to touch my cheekbone, and I flinch from the pain. Glancing in the mirror, I can see blood, and a bruise already forming.

But worse still are my attacker's words, still echoing in my head.

*"Your husband's power is slipping."*

I shake, my heart still pounding. This was what I was afraid of—that being linked to Nero would make me a target. But I was only thinking about the Feds, not criminal elements.

Who was she? What does she know?

And what happens now I have a target on my back?

## Chapter 7

## *Lily*

"I don't care what the fuck it takes, find who sent her!" Nero's angry roar fills the living room. It's barely an hour later, and we're back at the house – and we're not alone. The living room is full of people: Chase, Miles, a group of Nero's lieutenants, and a doctor, too, who checked my wound for glass and declared that I didn't need stitches. Now, I'm sitting on the couch with an ice pack on my face, watching Nero practically climb the walls.

"It's Kovak's people, it's got to be." Chase says, sending me a scowl. As if this is my fault. "She had a Russian accent."

"Maybe." I speak up. "It could have been something else."

Chase ignores me, focused on Nero again. "Sergei gave you a warning, didn't he? This is escalation."

"I'm not so sure," Miles, the nerdy-looking guy, speaks up. "A direct attack like this, on your wife. They'd have to know it means war."

"They're getting cocky." Chase argues. "Shit's getting out of hand. Are we really going to stand for this?"

Nero paces, radiating fury.

"Get the guys out, canvas the streets. Get me fucking answers. Like how the hell she knew we were there. Did someone at the restaurant tip them off? And tell Marco to check our hardware," he adds to Chase. "If this turns into a firefight, I want to know what we have in stock. You hear me?" he adds, raising his voice to the rest of them. "I want that bitch's name and who sent her by dawn, or I swear to God, I'll burn them all to the fucking ground."

I shiver at the violence in his voice.

His guys clear out, leaving us alone. I take a deep breath, trying to relax, but Nero is still pacing. He's barely looked at me since we got back.

"It's not a big deal," I speak up, my voice still shaky. "The doctor said, it won't even leave a scar."

"She touched you." Nero grinds out. "She dies."

I gulp. "And what about the guy who jostled me on the sidewalk?" I ask, trying to lighten the mood away from cold-blooded murder. "And the masseuse at the spa who pummeled my shoulders hard enough to leave marks? Are you going to put a price on their heads, too?"

Nero exhales sharply. "This isn't funny."

"I know," I swallow. "But please, Nero. Sit down. You're scaring me."

In an instant, he's on the couch beside me. He gently pulls the ice pack away from my face, and traces my bruised cheek.

"I'm so sorry, baby."

"Why?" I ask. "It's not your fault."

But we both know that's not exactly true. She hurt me to get to him. To send a message with the bruises she left on my face.

"They'll pay for this," he vows, and I believe him, even though I have no idea who 'they' are.

"I didn't even see her coming," I say, my voice cracking.

"I know," he leans forward, bringing his arms around me. I melt against him, and he holds me gently. Like I'm made of glass. "They're fucking cowards to the bone. Going after you instead of me. Attacking from behind..."

"And you think it's that guy from the party, Sergei...?"

He sighs. "Maybe. I honestly don't know just yet. It doesn't seem like their style but... Maybe Chase is right, they're getting cocky." He sees the questions in my eyes and explains: "The Kovaks are a Serbian gang, real bad son-of-a-bitches. We've had a kind of uneasy truce, going back years. You know, they stick to their side of the city, we stick to ours. But recently...? They're expanding. Trying to muscle in on our territory. And Barrettis don't stand for that shit."

I shiver again. Nero's kept me at arm's length from his criminal dealings since I arrived back in the city, and for the most part, I've been able to ignore them. Pretend like his life is all legit real estate deals and high-society functions—not a vast criminal empire, built on blood and crime.

But there's no ignoring it now. Not anymore.

"Don't worry," Nero says, holding me closer. "I'm going to keep you safe. I promise, nobody will touch you again."

I take a deep breath, comforted by the feeling of his arms around me. The one place I will always feel protected.

But after only a moment, he pulls away and gets to his feet. "I'll see you tomorrow," he says, heading for the door.

What?

"You're leaving?" I cry, leaping to my feet. "But you just said..."

"I'll sleep at the loft," Nero rakes a hand through his hair. "If they're coming for me, I won't have you getting caught in the crossfire."

"But..."

"It's safer this way," he insists, looking tortured. "*You'll* be safer. There are guards posted on the door," he adds. "One out back, too. I swear, nobody's getting in."

But that wasn't what I was protesting.

Nero moves back to me and drops a kiss on my forehead. "You're safe now," he whispers, and then he's gone too, and I'm alone in the house.

Wishing he was here, holding me instead.

After takeout and bad TV, I manage to fall asleep around two a.m., missing Nero's presence in the house. Even when we weren't speaking, I knew that he was right down the hall. Now, the house seems bigger. Emptier. And I'm rattling around, waiting for his call.

The next morning, I get dressed and kill time making pancakes from scratch.

*'When will I see you?'* I text Nero.

His reply bubbles on screen for what seems like an age, before it comes:

*'I've got to be at the club. I'm sending you something, though.'*

I'm just wondering what he means when I hear the doorbell. Wary, I go over to the window and peek out. Avery is standing on the porch. One of Nero's guards gives me a nod.

I open the door. "Hi," I say, cautious. We've never spent time together, at least, not one-on-one. And I still don't know about her close relationship with Nero.

Like just *how* close they are.

"Hey." Avery gives me an assessing look. She's dressed in cool-girl dark jeans, Doc Martin boots, and a leather jacket, her dark bangs choppy over black eyeliner. She looks tough, and ready for anything, and I... Do not.

I pull my fluffy robe tighter, self-conscious. "What are you doing here?" I ask, trying to sound polite.

"Nero sent me."

"Oh." I sigh. "Thanks, but I don't need a babysitter."

She smirks. "Good thing I'm not one. Go get dressed. We're spending the day together. Big plans."

I'm still tempted to refuse. But curiosity gets the better of me. I want to know her deal. And more about her history with Nero.

I open the door and invite her in. She pauses, sniffing the air.

"Do you want breakfast?" I offer, nodding to the kitchen. "I just made pancakes."

"See, just when I was prepared to hate you." Avery gives me a surprisingly friendly smile. "I'll eat, you dress. And none of those pretty dresses," Avery calls after me. "We're dressing for comfort, not the country club!"

I take Avery's advice, and wear jeans with a loose sweater and boots. She grabs a plate of pancakes for the road, and soon, we're speeding across the Brooklyn bridge in a sporty red Porsche.

"Nice car," I say admiringly.

"Nero loaned it," she replies, weaving through traffic like a NASCAR driver. "Nothing but the best for his Princess."

There's a faint edge to her voice, and I realize, that however suspicious I am of Avery, she's just as wary of me.

I look away. "So, where are we going for this big adventure?"

"You'll see," is all she says, and a few minutes later, we pull into a dusty parking lot beside...

"Eastern Guns and Ammo," I read from the sign. I blink. "A shooting range?"

Avery is already getting out of the car. "Now seems like a good time to learn how to handle a weapon, don't you think?"

It does. But I can't help looking at Avery with distrust. She seems to sense this because she meets my gaze head-on.

"Listen, let's clear the air, okay? I'm not fucking him."

I gape at her. "What?"

"That's the problem, right?" she smirks. "You're suspicious of me and Nero. Don't be. There's nothing like that between us, never has been. He's like a brother to me. A pig-headed, power-hungry, arrogant piece-of-shit brother," she adds affectionately. "So let's cut the catfight pick-me bullshit, and have some fun today, OK?"

"OK..." I echo slowly, as Avery strides to the door.

And dammit, now I really like her.

I hurry to catch up, and meet her at the counter, where a grizzled older guy outfits us with handguns and ammunition. Avery leads me to an aisle in the shooting range and shows me what to do.

"Safety. Clip. Bullets. Target." She loads the gun slowly, pointing out the parts, and lays it on the counter in front of me. "Think you've got it from here, Princess?"

"I'll try."

I put on the headset, and glass visor, and slowly pick up the gun. It's heavier than I expected and feels foreign in my hands as I raise it, pointing at the target.

"Feet apart," Avery instructs me. "Keep your weight low."

I aim.

BANG!

The handgun jerks in my hand when I pull the trigger, like a mini-explosion is going off. I stumble back, shocked.

Avery laughs. "Easy, there."

"Sorry." I blush. "Did I hit anything?"

"Just the backboard... Of the target next door." Avery grins.

"But don't worry, we'll make a marksman out of you in no time."

"Can you show me?" I ask.

"Sure." Avery steps up to the counter, loads and raises her gun in the blink of an eye, and aims.

BANG!

I can see the bullet hole torn through the middle of the target. A perfect shot.

"Wow," I applaud, impressed. "How did you learn to do that?"

"Same way you will: Practice." Avery steps aside. "Try it again, and this time, just squeeze the trigger gently. It won't take much force."

I do as she says, and this time, I manage to get the bullet on my own target. Way out to the side, but still!

"I did it!" I cheer. It's exhilarating.

More than that, it's empowering.

She laughs. "Fun, right? It's like meditation to me. You just focus on the target, and everything else melts away."

I shoot a couple more rounds, my aim improving with every shot. And my comfort, too.

"Do you think I'll need to use one of these?" I venture.

Avery shakes her head. "Not if Nero has anything to say about it. Damn, you should have seen him around the club this morning. Guy's just about ready to start a turf war as retribution for that black eye of yours."

I don't know whether to feel guilty for that, so I focus on my aim instead.

By the end of the morning, I'm feeling confident I could at least hit something right in front of me. "Good enough," Avery says. "Time for lunch."

She drives us to a fast food place, and we eat in the car,

devouring burgers and shakes, getting greasy wrappers all over the interior of Nero's Porsche.

Avery smirks, looking around. "Good thing you're here, Princess. He'd kill me to see this mess."

I pause, chewing on a fry. "How long have you been... Working with Nero?" I ask, wondering the right way to ask about her involvement with the Barrettis. Or even if there's a right way at all.

Avery slurps her milkshake. "My whole life," she replies, matter-of-fact. "My dad was one of Roman's guys, so I grew up in this world. He was killed when I was younger, and they looked out for us after that. My mom used to help run the legit businesses, they always need names without a criminal record," she explained, "for the liquor licenses, and taxes. She... Retired, a few years back, so when I turned eighteen, Nero brought me in to take over."

I can tell there's more to the story, but I don't push. "So you've known him a long time."

She nods. "I know he's got something brewing, something big. But these Kovaks... They don't fuck around."

I feel a chill. "Is he in danger?"

Avery gives me a dark smile. "He's Nero Barretti. Every morning he wakes up, a dozen people want him dead. And that's on a good day."

Back at the house, we walk inside to see that Nero is in the living room, with his lawyer, Miles. They are in the middle of what looks like an intense conversation when we come through the door, but it's cut off immediately.

They both fall silent.

"How did it go?" Nero asks, looking to Avery.

"Not bad," she replies.

"Are you kidding? I was amazing," I joke. "If there are any paper targets coming to get me, they better watch out."

Nero cracks a smile. "Good." He nods. "But it won't come to that. I'm keeping my guys here 24/7, indefinitely."

*But what about you?* I want to ask, but I keep my mouth shut.

"Anything I need to know?" Avery asks, her gaze moving to Miles.

"Like what?" he shoots back good-naturedly. "You already know everything."

"Damn right I do." She smiles, and her whole face softens for a moment.

I blink. Is something going on there?

But just as quickly, her cool-girl attitude shutters into place. "I'll give you a ride back to the club," Avery says, heading to the door. "The long way round, via Atlantic City."

"Hey!" Nero protests. "That's a valuable machine out there."

"Relax," Avery rolls her eyes. "I won't go over one-twenty."

She and Miles exit, leaving me alone with Nero.

He moves over to me. "How are you feeling?" he asks, searching my face.

He cups my cheek but doesn't touch my cheekbone. I know it looks bad. The bruise has turned an ugly brown and blue color that drew more than one curious stare while I was at the range with Avery.

"Fine. Better," I reassure him. "It doesn't hurt that much anymore."

"Still..." I can see the guilt in his eyes. "I'm so, so sorry, baby. I hate that you got hurt because of me."

I pull away. "Can you please stop treating me like I'm some helpless victim here?" I ask, my frustration over the past 24 hours finally breaking loose. "I was caught off-guard at the restaurant, but I promise that I'm not helpless. I've taken care of myself for a long time."

"But you didn't ask for any of this," Nero paces, looking fraught. "I put you in danger. I knew this could happen, and I shouldn't have—"

"No," I interrupt. "I chose this too. Coming back and *staying*. Even marrying you. I could have fought against you, refused to say the vows and taken my chances out in the world without you. But I didn't. I chose you!"

Nero shakes his head angrily. "No."

"Yes." I move closer, determination pounding in my veins. And maybe it's my day at the gun range, taking aim, feeling the power flow through me, but I'm sick of playing catchup. Being the one reacting to everyone else's choices instead of having my own way.

Just for once, I want to call the shots.

And I need him. *Bad*.

"I chose you," I repeat it again. "I *want* you."

I boldly put my hands on his chest and push him back onto the couch behind him. Nero sinks back, even though I know I'm no match for his strength. "What do you want?" he mutters, looking tortured. His hands clenched in fists at his sides, like he's holding himself back from me—even when I straddle his lap.

He makes a groaning sound, hips bucking up against me of their own accord. "Fuck, Lily... I'm trying to keep you safe here."

"So stop pushing me away." I lean in and drop a kiss on his cheek. His earlobe. The corner of his mouth. I grind in his lap, drawing another fevered curse from his lips. "I'm safest when I'm with you. I know you'd never let anyone hurt me. I want you," I whisper again. "Please, Nero... Don't make me beg. Unless you want me to...?" I draw back and give him a seductive pout. "I'll do it, on my knees for you, I'll beg for your cock—"

His mouth swallows my words, a desperate, passionate kiss. Nero's arms go around me, his hands going up the back of my shirt and sunning over my bare skin. I shiver to his touch, grinding in his lap again, where I can feel the hard ridge of his erection pressed between my legs, where a pulsing desire is burning out of control.

After days of aching for him, it feels incredible to have his hands on me. His mouth.

*I'm right where I belong.*

I pull back and go for the hem of my shirt, yanking it over my head and tossing it away. Nero doesn't wait for permission before unhooking my bra and getting rid of it too. My back arches, thrusting my breasts forward into his face. I push them together with my hands, the pink peaks of my nipples front and center for his mouth.

He lavishes them, sucking and licking like a man possessed. I moan. God, the feeling of his tongue slaving over the sensitive skin is electric, making every inch of my body coming alive. I grind again, rocking back and forth against the ridge of his erection, and even through his jeans, I can feel him grow harder. Thicker. As I chase the friction of contact, wet heat pooling right there.

*Fuck.* The things this man can do to me...

I reach between us, unfastening my jeans and shoving them down, then popping his fly open too. His erection bursts out, right there between us, and I fist it in my hands as I ride his lap. My panties are soaked through, and I'm moaning, loving the feel of his thick head bumping up against my clit with every dirty grind.

"Making a mess of me, Princess?" Nero groans, lifting his head from my breasts. His eyes are dark, glazed with lust, and

God, it only makes me grind again. "You just going to rub that wet pussy all over my stiff dick, or be a good girl, and put it all the way inside?"

I shudder at the filthy words, my excitement growing to a fever pitch.

"Inside," I gasp. "I need you inside me, *now*."

I stand to tear off the rest of my clothes as Nero yanks his jeans all the way off.

"Take it, baby," he growls, leaning back against the cushions with his thick cock rearing up from his lap. "Ride it like you own it. Because fuck, it's all yours."

I straddle him again, and then, holding his eyes, I lower myself onto his cock.

"Fuck..."

He hisses through his teeth, hands going to grip my fleshy thighs as I let out my own gasp of pleasure. "You feel so good," I whimper, bearing down all the way until he's buried inside me, right to the hilt.

I clench, and feel his whole body stiffen. "You feel that?" I ask, gripping again.

"Like heaven," he groans. "Your tight little cunt is fucking heaven on earth."

I lean in, loving the control I have in this position. Seeing this big, powerful man come undone.

"Then say your prayers," I coo, arching my back. "Because I haven't even started yet."

I work myself up and down on his cock, riding to the tip and back down to the base. And then again, faster.

"Fuck, Princess..." Nero growls again, gripping my thighs tighter. "Just like that, baby."

He spears up inside me, and I whimper, tossing my head back. The friction of his thick cock is incredible, and everything else fades away. The conflicts in our marriage, the attack last night, the uncertain future.

None of that matters.

I can only care about the feel of his body, and the pleasure that's driving me closer and closer to my climax. I don't know how I've gotten by for so long without this feeling, the passion that only this man can bring out of me.

"Look at you," Nero gazes up at me as I ride him. Panting. Groaning. "The most gorgeous goddamn sight in the world. They could come for me right now, and I wouldn't stop. I'd die with my dick inside you, and fuck, I'd die a happy man."

SMACK.

I slap him across the face before I can stop myself. "Don't you dare talk about dying," I exclaim, my heart pounding. Nero catches my hand with a snarl, eyes flashing.

"My baby wants it rough?"

In an instant, he's lifted me, spun around, and fucked me deep into the couch.

I scream with pleasure, suddenly beneath him.

"My girl's got fire in her belly, huh?" He pistons into me again, bracing one hand on the couch back above us, gripping it for purchase as he thrusts into me, harder.

Deeper.

*Fuck.*

"Yeah, I see it," Nero growls, gripping my jaw in his other hand. Eyes burning dark. Frenzied with an animal lust. "You love to ride it, bounce those pretty tits for me, but this is what you need to get you there. You need to be owned, to feel my cock drilling so goddamn deep you won't walk tomorrow without feeling every inch."

He slams again, a punishing rhythm that makes me sob with ecstasy.

"Say it," he demands. "Say you need your man giving it to you good."

"Yes!" I cry, my body jolting with the force of impact every time he thrusts. "Yes, Nero! God, I love it. I love it when you fuck me. Don't stop!"

"Never," he growls, grinding up, finding that perfect spot, right there, the one that makes me wail. "Got to give it to my Princess real deep. Because it's not the goddamn ring on your finger that says you belong to me, it's the way your pussy holds on tight and won't let go."

He angles deep again, pressing my clit and stroking my inner walls all at once. "*Mine.*"

I come with a howl, his name falling from my lips as my core tightens. I dig my fingernails into his back and hold on for dear life, pleasure shattering through me.

But he doesn't stop. Nero fucks me through my orgasm, and into the next, pistoning relentlessly with perfect pitch, until I'm sobbing, clawing at him, my body convulsing like never before. It's too much, too much to take, but he just keeps giving it to me, over and over until he rears up with an animal roar, pulling out of me, and fisting his cock in his hand, spurting his climax down all over my naked body.

Marking his claim.

*Oh my God.*

I watch in a lusty daze as his face slackens, the hot liquid painting my skin. It's the sexiest thing, like he's paying tribute to me. Worshipping me. And I see it in his eyes, the power I have over him.

*I did this.*

Nero collapses forward with a groan, pulling me into his arms, despite the mess. I lay there against him, sticky and breathless, reeling from another epic orgasm, burying my face in his neck as I slowly come back down to earth.

I can't help but giggle.

Nero barely lifts his head, eyes still shut. "If you're laughing, I did something wrong. Give me five minutes, and I'll have you screaming instead."

"No, it's not that." I smile, nestling closer. "I was just thinking... Every time, it's the best I've ever had. And then you go and raise the bar again."

I feel the rumble of his laughter in his chest. "Like I said, give me five, and I'll have you screaming."

He strokes my hair, and I feel a wash of calm roll over me. It's not just the endorphins bringing me such an unexpected sense of peace. What I said before, I meant it: I chose Nero. Despite everything that's happened, I stand by that choice. The connection between us is too strong to ignore, and every time I try, I end up right back here where I started:

In his arms.

There's no hiding it or denying things that my heart already knows to be true. Annulment, divorce, even walking out and disappearing for good... They're not real options to me, not anymore. I've made my choice. It's Nero, every time.

And now I'm going to figure a way to live with that.

# Chapter 8

## *Lily*

I wake the next day with a new determination in my bloodstream. Nero heads into the office, making me promise to keep Kyle close as my new official bodyguard, leaving me in our bed, watching the sun stream through the windows. My words from last night echo, and I turn them all over in my mind.

For the first time, I'm owning my choices. I'm not a helpless victim here. And if this is my life, then I need to ask myself: What do I want? It's easy to focus on the physical with Nero, our passion is overwhelming, but it goes much deeper than that. I have a chance for a future here. I could maybe find real happiness, and I'm not just focusing on my relationship with Nero when it comes to that.

Back before all this drama started, when I could allow myself to dream, there was more that I wanted for myself. A home, a career, a chance to pursue my passion... That got lost under the mess of Witness Protection, and then the years in hiding, scraping by to support Teddy.

I thought my dreams were out of reach.

But what if they're not?

\* \* \*

"And if you'll come this way, I can show you the new digital media wing..."

My heels click on the polished floors, as I follow my guide down the hallway. My nerves are tangled in my stomach as I look around at open doorways, revealing classes in progress and studio space. It only took a quick call to Marissa to be connected to a woman she knows in the Alumni office at the Newton School of Art, a school just a couple of blocks from Washington Square Park. They're a college-level program, but they have a massive extended education program too, offering classes on everything from portraiture to sculpting- and digital media.

The school had always been on my dream college list, back when I was in school. Now, as I walk the halls, touring the buildings, that same sense of possibility sparkles in my veins.

"Is there a particular discipline you're interested in?" The woman asks, friendly.

I gulp, self-conscious about my lack of experience. "I... Well, my background is in painting. Oils, watercolor. But I'd love to learn new things."

"Well, we take an interdisciplinary approach here," the woman says. "We encourage you to sample classes widely and experiment out of your comfort zone. You never know what new media you'll connect with—or how those new skills can broaden and enrich your core work."

"That sounds amazing."

She shows me around the photography department, with an incredible exhibition on display. Plus the ceramics studio, the lecture halls, the library.... The facilities are state of the art, and I know that I can learn how to be the best artist possible here.

*If* they accept me.

"But, since your passion is canvas..." my guide pushes another door open and beckons me inside. "This is probably where you'll be spending your time."

I walk inside and look around. The space is large and open. There are empty easels set up everywhere in a semi-circle around a large platform.

"Hello?" a voice says, and I turn to see a woman emerge from a washroom in back.

She's wearing a navy apron with paint splatters all over it. Her brown hair is pulled back, and her eyes are the color of honey. She looks so familiar, but I can't place her. I'm sure we've never met.

"Oh, Professor Keene," the tour guide says, seeming flustered. "I'm sorry to interrupt. I didn't know you were here."

"It's perfectly fine," the professor says. She has a kind smile. "I'm just cleaning out the paintbrushes and palettes. People tend to underestimate how important it is to keep everything clean in a paint studio," she adds, with a teasing grin. "It can ruin an artist's day when the muse strikes, but they have to stop to prepare their equipment. I often wonder how many great pieces of art have faded into the ether because an artist couldn't hold onto inspiration while washing out their paint brushes."

I laugh. I like this woman.

"I'm Lily," I say, giving a small wave as the woman wipes her wet hands off on a towel.

"Miranda Keene," she replies, and my jaw drops.

Now, I know why she looks familiar. Miranda Keene is a huge name in the art world. Her paintings are beautiful.

"*The* Miranda Keene?"

She's chuckles. "Probably not the only one in the world, but I am the artist, if that's what you're referring to."

Of course, she is.

"I'm sorry," I blurt. "I'm just surprised. I didn't realize the teachers here were, well, like you."

"There are several working artists here," she says, and I make a mental note to look that up on the school's website later. "I only have time for teach a couple of classes a week, but I like passing along my wisdom to aspiring artists. You never know what kind of discovery can be made by helping others do what you do. It's very satisfying. Are you a new student?"

"Maybe," I reply. "I mean, I hope to be."

"Well, good luck," she says with a wink. "Perhaps I'll see you in my class soon."

"I would like that," I manage to reply, face burning. Like it? I'd love it!

The guide steers me out, smiling at my starstruck expression. "Don't worry, you get used to it," she confides. "My first week, I could barely talk in class, I was so intimidated. But everyone's friendly. It's a great community. Did you need any more information?"

I shake my head. "I have everything," I say, clutching the brochures she gave me. "The application is right here."

"Good luck!"

I'm going to need it. I'm sitting at a café nearby leafing through the pages, wondering if my portfolio even stands a chance, when Juliet arrives to meet me for lunch.

"Hey!" she greets me happily, wearing a loose boxy dress and big sunglasses. "You look great."

"You mean, aside from my shiner?" I ask.

"I was going to be tactful and wait until we at least had fries before asking about that," she winces. "What happened?"

"Would you believe a bathroom brawl?" I say, making light of it.

Juliet gives me a concerned look, like she knows there's more to it than that. "Nero must be thrilled."

I chuckle. "Yeah, he's gone into full caveman protector mode. Which, I hate to admit, is kind of hot."

Juliet smirks. "I won't tell if you don't. Caleb nearly lost his mind when someone drove me off the road. And then there was the time his stalker tried burning our cabin down..."

I choke on my ice water. "And here I was, thinking you guys were a boring high society couple."

"Oh, I have stories," she twinkles, putting me at ease. Underneath her sweet exterior, Juliet is clearly made of sterner stuff. No wonder she doesn't flinch around Nero.

"So," she prompts, after we order. "How do you like the ring?"

I glance down. "I love it," I admit. "I take it I have you to thank for picking it out?"

She shakes her head. "Nope, that's all Nero. He must have looked at a hundred of them before picking it out. He wanted it to be perfect."

I feel a glow. "Well, it is."

"Almost as good as mine," Juliet says with a smirk, flashing her own amazing ring, and we laugh.

She notices the application packet beside my plate and picks it up. "What's this?"

I explain briefly to her about my tour of the Newton school. Juliet looks excited.

"Really? You want to go back to school?"

I nod. "It's an old dream," I explain. "One that's been on

hold for about ten years. So, I just decided... I don't want to wait anymore."

"That's really great! You've got to pursue your passions," she says. "It's easy for them to take a backseat with everything else going on. I mean, I love Caleb, but drama seems to follow the man around," she adds with a mischievous grin. "And I'm guessing Nero is just the same."

I smile. I know exactly what she means. "He's like... a black hole," I say. "Pulling everything into his orbit. A force of nature."

"Bingo." Juliet laughs, as our plates arrive. She pauses, wincing at her food. "I'm sorry," she murmurs to the waitress. "I asked for the tuna to be cooked well done. I can't eat it rare."

"Of course." Her plate is whisked away.

I pause. She didn't order wine, either. No alcohol, no raw fish...

Is she pregnant?

My curiosity burns but I bite my tongue. It's probably early days, she's not even showing, and I don't want to pry. But it gives new weight to her words about finding her own life, outside of her relationship. She and Caleb have managed to build a life together, despite tumultuous beginnings.

It gives me hope that Nero and I could do the same.

But just when I'm beginning to relax, and think of the future, the real world intrudes. We've finished lunch, and I'm leaving the café with Juliet when I spot a light grey sedan parked across the street.

I'm not sure, but I think I remember seeing it outside the Newton School, earlier today.

"What's up?" Juliet asks, noticing I've stopped.

I shake my head. "Nothing. I'll see you soon. For that double date," I joke, and she laughs.

"Stay safe!"

I meet Kyle at the curb, where he's been casually waiting with eyes on our patio table, all along.

"You see that car down the block?" I ask, climbing in the backseat. "The grey one?"

Kyle checks it in the mirror without turning. A pro. "You've seen it before?"

I nod. "Maybe."

"I'll take care of it." He eases away from the curb, passing the car as we head down the street. I quickly glance to see who's inside, and find two men up front, dark-haired and heavyset.

Our eyes meet, and I shiver, whipping my head away.

Who are they?

It could be the Feds, still watching me, but it could be someone else, too. *The Kovaks.* They had to be keeping tabs on Nero and me to approach me in that bathroom, after all.

Behind us, the sedan eases into traffic, and follows us through the lights.

I gulp. "They're following us," I tell Kyle. Suddenly, I'm very glad to have him behind the wheel.

"Not for long, they won't be."

Heading into heavy traffic, he changes lanes suddenly, making his way from one side of the road to the other with no turn signal. I see the grey sedan struggling to keep up. Then, a stop light in front of us turns yellow. The cars around us start to slow, but Kyle hits the gas and flies through the light just as it turns red.

The grey sedan tailing us is stuck behind a pickup truck, several cars back.

Kyle quickly yanks the wheel, sending us speeding down an alleyway, into the next street, and then along a dizzying route that even I can't follow, until finally, we pull up outside the club.

I exhale. "Did Nero recruit you from NASCAR?" I ask, reeling. "Or did Avery give you driving lessons?"

Kyle cracks the first smile I've ever seen on his burly face. "I'm the one who taught her," he says. "Bitch stole all my moves."

I laugh, heading inside. For the first time, Nero's protection feels like a relief, rather than a prison. I know I'm safe here, surrounded by his guys, and I move confidently through the club into the back, to his office.

"Knock, knock," I push his door open, and find him deep in paperwork. I hold up the takeout bag I brought from lunch. "They had an Italian sub on the menu. I know nothing lives up to Gino's, but..."

Nero's stressed expression melts into a smile. "You brought me lunch."

"Don't get used to it," I warn him with a smirk, depositing it on the desk.

"Any problems?" he asks, unwrapping the food.

I wince, and quickly explain about our suspected tail. "But it might not have been anything!" I exclaim. "I was probably just overreacting."

"Or the Kovaks have someone on you now." He scowls.

"Kyle lost them, it's fine," I reassure him. I move around the desk, and Nero pulls me into his lap.

"I hate the thought of you out there, without me," he says, breathing me in.

"Well, short of locking me up at the house all day, there's nothing to do," I reply, wriggling on his lap.

"Don't tempt me," Nero grumbles, and I smile.

"Been there, done that. Didn't turn out too well for either of us," I remind him.

He sighs. "I know."

I kiss him, enjoying the feel of his strong hands locked around my waist. Finally, we come up for air.

"There's actually something I wanted to talk to you about..." I start, suddenly nervous.

"So the food was to butter me up?" Nero smirks.

"Maybe." I smile back. "Before lunch... I went to tour an art school. I want to take classes there—if they accept me."

I show him the brochure, and explain about the course I could follow, my excitement returning as I describe the buildings and teachers. "It could be amazing," I say.

"So what are you waiting for? Do it," he says immediately.

"I have to submit a portfolio," I say. "And be accepted into the program."

"That won't be a problem. You're an incredible artist."

I glow. "And then... Well, there's tuition."

Nero bursts out laughing. "That's what you're worried about?"

"What?" I protest, blushing. "It's not cheap."

Nero lifts me off his lap and walks over to the safe on the far wall. He keys in a code, and swings open the door, revealing stack after stack of banded cash. He tosses one down, and then then next. And another.

"Nero!" I protest.

"What?" he grins. "In case you haven't noticed, cash isn't exactly in short supply around here."

"But still. That's your money."

"Bullshit." Nero strides back to me, pulling me close. "We took vows, remember, baby? What's mine is yours. And what's yours is mine."

I roll my eyes. "I have nothing. Or like, a hundred bucks to my name, total."

"Not anymore. You're my wife," Nero insists, eyes glittering down at me. "And it's time you started acting like it. You don't need to come to me, asking permission, like you're on some fucking allowance. You want it? It's yours."

I suck in a breath, exhilarated. "So, tuition is OK?"

"If it puts that smile on your face, I'll buy the whole fucking school for you."

I laugh. "That won't be necessary," I say, throwing my arms around his neck. "Thank you."

"Nothing to thank me for, Princess." Nero kisses me. "But if you insist... I can think of a few ways..."

When did that nickname change from a taunting sneer to a term of endearment? I can't be sure, but I like it. Every time he calls me that now, I feel like he's telling me I'm precious to him.

"What did you have in mind?" I arch closer, deepening the kiss. Nero's masculine groan rumbles against my lips, and he grabs my ass with both hands, massaging my cheeks through the thin fabric of my sundress.

"You look so hot in that thing," he growls, tearing away. "How about you bend over my desk and let me get that pussy nice and wet?"

Desire shoots through me. I'm just about to turn around and do exactly what he's asking when voices come from outside the office, angry and loud.

Nero steps away from me, just as Chase storms in, with Miles and another tall, shaven-headed guy hot on their tail.

"What the fuck's going on?" Nero demands, suddenly all business again.

They crowd in, and I step back, out of the way.

"The shipment got busted," Chase says.

"What?" Nero exclaims. "How?"

"Feds came out of nowhere," he says. "Our guys didn't stand a chance. They've got them in custody."

"Fuck!" Nero slams his fist on the table, so loud I flinch. "*Fuck.*"

"What do you want to do, boss?" Miles looks anxious. "I can get down there, try to bail them out ASAP, but I'm guessing the Feds won't make it easy."

Nero paces, dragging a hand through his hair. "Wait. Give me a minute to think."

The shaven-headed one steps up, finally speaking. "You better think fast, Barretti. Because clearly, the Feds are all over this organization. And they'll be coming for you next."

My heart plummets.

*Shit.*

## Chapter 9

### *Nero*

This is a fucking nightmare.

There's chaos following Vance's announcement, but I'm quick to fall into leader mode. There are too many people here for this to be a productive meeting, so I quickly send all but the essentials packing, leaving just Vance, Chase, and Miles.

Lily hovers, trying to make herself look inconspicuous. Fat chance. If she's here, I won't be able to focus on anyone else, and with the Feds closing in, I can't take the risk.

"You need to leave," I tell her, steering her to the door.

"But I want to stay," she protests. "Maybe I can help."

"With what?" I say bluntly. "This isn't your shit to deal with. Go."

She gives me a look. "What's yours is mine," she whispers, so nobody else can hear. Throwing my words right back at me.

It won't change my mind. "Kyle!" I yell, and he materializes in the hallway. "Take her home," I order him. "Eyes on your tail. And tell the guys at the house, no slacking off tonight. If a hobo pisses in the gutter, they pay attention 'til he's done."

He nods. Lily looks frustrated, but she follows him out. I slam the door behind them and turn to the group.

"OK," I take a deep breath, getting my head in the fucking game. Rival gangs, Feds closing in... it's all happening at once, and I need to think straight. "Tell me exactly what happened. Start at the beginning, and don't leave anything out."

"It was a normal delivery," Chase says. "Guys at the docks gave the all-clear, so Benny and Tito went in like normal to unload the crate. Then I get a call, ten minutes ago maybe, our guy on the watch tower says the Feds swooped in, swept them up."

"They had to have had a tip," Vance speaks up. He's lounging on the couch in the corner, scratching his damn balls like this is casual chitchat.

I tense. "No way. This place is locked down. My guys don't narc."

"So how do you explain it?" he asks, still so cool. "They knew exactly where you'd be, which container to hit. That's not a lucky bust, that's intel."

I glare. I don't want him here, sticking his nose in my business, but I know, he's got a direct line to my father.

I need to be smart. Show no weakness. I need to be the fucking Barretti boss.

"I told you to take a break with the imports," I turn to Chase. "Keep us a low profile."

"This was supposed to be one of the last," he says defensively, but it doesn't help. "No hassle, just a couple more deliveries."

"Yeah, and how'd that turn out?" I demand, my anger rising. "That bullshit's a liability! And now you've left us exposed, right when I need shit running smoothly for the development."

## Ruthless Games

"So, what are we supposed to do?" he says stubbornly. "Cede our territory to the fucking Kovaks?"

I get up in his face. "You're supposed to follow my orders."

Chase backs up, but just a little.

"It was probably them, narcing to the FBI. I bet you they're the ones who tipped them off. Set us up, to fuck with our shipments and send a message."

I look to Miles. He shrugs. "Could be," he says. "Barretti men go down, they win."

I pace, frustrated.

"I want damage control," I spit out. Soon enough, this whole operation will be legit, and I don't have to worry about petty street shit like this, but until that day comes... "Miles, get down to the courthouse, see about making bail."

"Feds won't give that up easy," Vance speaks up again. "They'll be leaning on them hard to flip. We should take care of them first chance we get."

"What? Absolutely not," I shake my head. "My guys are solid."

"You sure about that?"

"Yes." I stare him down. "They won't fold. Feds will have nothing but a couple of delivery guys, and hell, who knows if they even got their warrants straight? Miles, get a copy of the documents, see if you can work your magic."

"Yes boss," he leaves.

"Chase, talk to our guys at the docks. See when the Feds started sniffing around. And for God's sake, shut the rest of it down. I mean it," I add, my voice like steel. "We're hitting pause on everything until this shit's figured out."

"But—" he starts to protest.

I silence him with a look. "You heard me. If there's a mole around here, we're not going to hand them another bust on a platter. Shut. It. Down."

Chase sighs, but he nods, and clears out.

"And what's my homework, *boss?*" Vance asks with a smirk.

"I don't fucking care."

I stride past him, through the club, until I can shove open a back exit and emerge into the fresh air.

Fuck. *Fuck.*

I pace in the back alleyway, my head spinning. This is the last thing I need right now. I'm so close to getting us out of this, all the seedy deals and illegal shit that have made up the Barretti empire for so long.

I want a clean slate. Not just for me and Lily, but for my crew, too. No more Feds sniffing around, no more risk of prison or violence just to get through another day. I've been slowly making my moves in secret for years, we've finally broken ground on the development, and now this?

A Fed/Kovak one-two punch. But I won't go down for the count.

My phone goes off in my pocket, and I pull it out, hoping it's not more bad news. It's a text from Lily.

*'Remember, the fundraiser tonight. 8pm.'*

Christ, it's the last thing I need: Putting on a tux and glad-handing a bunch of bigwigs.

But they're the bigwigs I need. Developers. Bankers. Politicians.

Ian McKenna was only the beginning. Now we're up and running on the project, I need it to be smooth sailing all the way.

*'Meet you there,'* I text back. For a moment, I wish we could blow it off. Go lose myself in her touch and the hot grip of her sweetness, making everything go away.

But I'm Nero fucking Barretti. The buck stops with me. So I put my phone away, go back inside, and start fixing shit. And then I put on a tuxedo, and head over to the party, like this entire empire isn't hanging in the balance.

"Hey," Lily greets me by the doors, looking concerned. She's gorgeous in a floor-length gown, green silk making her hair shine gold. "What happened? Is everything OK?"

"It's fine," I reply, nodding to the doorman as we head inside.

"But Chase seemed really stressed," she keeps pushing. "Is it Agent Greggs, or someone else? Are your guys OK?—"

"I said, it's fine." I cut her off, too harsh. "I can't deal with it here. Let's just get through tonight."

Frustration flashes on her face. "I'm supposed to be your partner in this," she says. "We took vows, remember? Or have they already slipped your mind?"

"Lily." My voice is warning.

"I just hate it when you shut me out."

I tense. Why can't she see that I'm doing this for her own good? The less she knows about the Barretti empire, the better.

Luckily, we're interrupted by some society types she knows, and she has to quickly hide her mood with a smile. "Robert! Lucinda, so lovely to see you. And for such a good cause!"

I've never been glad of the social small talk, but right now, it's great timing. I grab a glass of wine from a passing waiter and look around. I'm used to being met with scandalized stares and disapproval at a place like this, but I'm surprised to see more people look curious or impressed instead.

Guess a billion-dollar project will do that to a man's reputation.

I'm glad. Not because I give a shit, but because Lily deserves better than gossip and scorn. She deserves the best.

"... We'll have to catch up soon," Lily is trilling. "But right now, I need to steal my husband away. See you!"

She steers me away, out to the gardens. I'm still feeling a stab of pride hearing her refer to me as her husband when she whirls on me, deadly serious.

"Will the Feds come after you for this bust? Do you have an alibi?" she asks.

*No.*

"Lily, let it go. We should enjoy the party," I say, refusing to keep talking about this with her. If I had my way, no aspect of this life would ever touch her. Maybe if I was less of a selfish asshole, I'd be able to just let her go and be safe away from me.

But I also have the sneaking suspicion that she wouldn't leave, anyway.

We're drawn to each other like moths to a flame. It's always been like this.

"No, I won't just smile and pretend everything's OK." she insists, and I grit my teeth. She can never just make something easy.

She can never let anything go. She always has to push me until I'm mad.

"What do you mean, no?" I ask, taking her arm and pulling her away from the more crowded part of the party.

"I'm tired of being kept in the dark!" she exclaims, anger flashing in her eyes. "It's a bad idea anyway. I never would have talked to Sergei if I'd known that he was your enemy. And the attack at the restaurant? Maybe I would have been more alert if you didn't keep me in the dark all the time."

That's a low blow.

"Stay out of it, Lily," I warn. "This is your world, *this* one," I growl, gesturing around. "Not down in the filth with me."

"But—" Lily starts to argue, but then she pauses, looking past me. Confusion and fear mar her face.

I turn.

It's the Feds. Swarming the party, the whole damn SWAT team out in force. Everyone stops to stare, eyes wide.

"Nero?" Lily's voice shakes.

"Don't worry," I tell her, even as that smug bastard agent strolls over. The one who was meeting behind my back with Lily. He's got a shit-eating grin on his face, and a warrant in his hand.

"Nero Barretti."

"That's me," I act casual, sipping my wine. "Great party, huh? You need to try the little crab puff things. Delicious."

He rolls his eyes, whips out the cuffs, and slams me against the wall. As he reads me my rights, I catch Lily's eyes. She's watching, stricken.

Fuck.

I want to comfort her, but there's no time.

"Call Miles," I call, as they roughly hustle me away. "It'll be fine. I promise."

I just have to hope it's a promise I can keep.

## Chapter 10

### *Lily*

I'm frozen in place as I watch the FBI take Nero away. Greggs is among the arresting officers, but he doesn't look my way once. I almost expect to be taken as well. Instead, I'm left standing there in the middle of the garden, clutching my purse.

All eyes are on me, but I can't make myself care about that. I'm too busy teetering between panic and fear. I can't believe that I just watched Nero being arrested. I knew that the situation was serious at the club earlier—the tension in the air was thick enough to cut with a knife—but I had no idea the fallout would be so swift.

He must have been arrested because of the raid earlier today. I didn't catch many details before Nero hustled me out, but it turns out that the tattooed man was right.

They came for Nero next.

And now I have to do something.

I turn and head for the exit, leaving the gossip and gasps behind. I couldn't care less what anyone thinks about us now. All that matters is Nero, and getting him free.

I find Kyle waiting in the car. He takes me straight to the club, but it's not until I walk in that I remember I'm still wearing a floor-length gown.

Fuck it.

I throw open his office door, and find Chase there, deep in conversation with a couple of other guys.

He stands, surprised. "What the—"

"Nero's been arrested," I announce.

He curses.

"They took him at the party, in front of everyone. They wanted to send a message," I add, furious.

To humiliate him in front of everyone. Remind him he'll always be part of the criminal underworld. I know Agent Greggs' game, but I'm not playing.

Not this time.

"He said to call Miles," I add. Chase nods to someone, who whips out their phone and calls.

"Thanks for letting us know," Chase says shortly. "Leave it to us."

He turns his back, shutting me out again, but I'm not standing for it now.

"No," I say firmly, making them all look up. "I'm staying."

"Look, Princess—"

"We both know, I have a target on my back," I speak over him. "From the Kovaks, hell, from you guys too. If Nero ends up in jail, there goes my protection. My ass is on the line now. You can't keep me out of this."

I stand tall, even though I'm quaking inside. Talk back to these men? They could kill me with their bare hands. And probably have a few bodies to their names.

There's a moment of awkward tension, and everyone exchanges an intense look. But still, Chase sneers. "What are you going to do?" he asks, dismissive. "You're just his wife."

"Exactly." I scowl. "I'm his family now. So tell me everything."

There's another long silence, and then the bald guy, Vance, I think his name is, lays out the situation. The FBI, or DEA, or someone raided their delivery meet. Two guys are already in custody, and the Feds are probably leaning on them, hard.

"They don't want a couple of low-level grunts," he says, regarding me with cool eyes. I shiver. I don't trust him, and I've never heard Nero mention his name, but for now, I need to make nice with everyone. "They want the boss. To get enough on Nero to take down this whole organization."

"If you haven't already given them enough to work with," Chase mutters.

I ignore him.

I have a plan forming in my mind, and it's a hell of a risk, but I have to take it. Nero cannot be charged with anything, or I have no doubt that my own head will end up on a chopping block, too.

It's enough to terrify me, but I'm going to keep my wits together.

"OK." I say, getting to my feet. "I know what I need to do."

"And what's that, Princess?" Chase sneers, as I head for the door.

I turn, and level him a glare. "Since you guys are content to sit around here on your asses, I'm going to do what you all can't. I'm going to get my husband back."

*  *  *

First thing the next morning, I'm sitting in an interview room at the FBI offices in midtown. I haven't slept a wink, but I make sure I look the part: a crisp white blazer over a matching mini-skirt, my hair sleek and blow-dried, perfect makeup and tasteful jewelry. I look every inch the society sweetheart, and I plan to use that image like a weapon.

"Can we get you anything?" the junior agent waiting with me asks. He's been staring at my legs since I walked in, so I smile, like butter wouldn't melt.

"Aren't you a doll? I'd just love some coffee, if you don't mind. Two sugars, cream?"

"I... Sure," he blurts, looking flustered.

"Miles?" I ask, turning to the man beside me. There's no way I was walking in here unprotected. And if Nero trusts him, that's good enough for me. "Coffee?"

He looks thrown. "Uh, sure. Thanks."

"I'll be right back." The agent darts out, and I exhale, collecting myself.

"Nero won't be happy," Miles mumbles, looking nervously around. "He said to keep you far away from this mess."

"Well, we can't always get what we want, can we?" I say, determined not to waver from my plan.

I look around. We're in a brightly lit, windowless room with nothing but a metal table and chairs inside. And a mirror on the wall, of course. It's got to be a one-way mirror, just like in a bad cop movie. I can imagine some higher-up in a suit standing on the other side of the glass, watching as we chat.

"So, how was your weekend?" I ask pleasantly.

Miles boggles.

"Lily..."

"Just making conversation," I say, trying to ignore the nerves fluttering in my stomach.

I need to be an ice queen. Fucking unmovable.

The door suddenly swings open, and a stern-faced woman enters. She's in her fifties, maybe, wearing a severe black pantsuit, with her dark hair pulled back in a low bun. She's all business, giving me a sharp look.

"Lily Barretti?" she asks briskly

"That's me," I answer with a bright smile. I offer my hand. "So lovely to meet you, Ms...?"

"Agent Lydia Compton," she corrects me.

"Lydia! What a lovely name," I coo. "One of my girlfriends named her daughter that. Did you know it means, father's joy?"

She looks at me like I'm crazy, but it's all part of my plan. The more they underestimate me, the simpler this will be.

"You do understand why you're here?" she asks slowly, like I'm an idiot.

I keep smiling. "To help with this mix-up," I reply brightly. "I'm sure we can get the misunderstanding about my husband all cleared up."

She mutters something under her breath, rolling her eyes as Agent Greggs walks in, joining us.

"Lily," he nods, taking a seat at the table, but everything about his body language tells me he's not calling the shots now. This woman must be his boss.

"Now that we're all here..." Lydia places a brown manila envelope on the table.

"Not quite." I stop her. "I'm actually still waiting on my coffee."

Two incredulous faces stare back at me.

"I hope you realize how serious this situation is, Mrs. Barretti. You're connected to a very dangerous man."

I give a trill of a laugh. "Like I said, it's a misunderstanding. Nero wouldn't hurt a fly."

Lydia opens the folder. Surveillance photos, trained on the club and some warehouses. They show Nero, mostly entering and exiting with various people. Chase... Avery... even me.

"What am I supposed to be looking at?" I ask, still smiling, as Miles sits beside me, making notes.

"A criminal conspiracy." Lydia glares. "Guns, drugs, money laundering."

"Really? But I don't see him with any guns. Or drugs. It just looks like a legitimate business organization to me." I push the photos back to them. "Nero Barretti is a respected entrepreneur."

Lydia looks impatient. "We arrested these men yesterday." She points a red manicured finger at a picture of men in a warehouse. "And they work directly for your husband."

"Is that what they've told you?" I ask. Her face doesn't flinch.

"You know your husband isn't an innocent man in all this," Lydia snaps. "He's taken over his father's position as leader of the Barretti organization, and we all know it."

Miles clears his throat. "I have to protest this ongoing harassment of Mr. Barretti," he says.

"Disrupting his social engagements, making a display of his arrest instead of simply inviting him for an interview. If you had any evidence, you would have charged him by now. Have you?"

"We have up to seventy-two hours to charge him." Agent Greggs says, but his reply makes my nerves ease a little.

*They don't have anything.*

The realization sinks in. Miles is right. There's no direct evidence. Nero's men haven't turned on him.

They're fishing here.

I try to hide my relief. "Did you want to take my statement?" I ask, sounding bored. "Because I have a manicure booked at ten, I don't want to miss it."

"This isn't a joke," Lydia seethes. This woman is a real ballbuster. I can see why Greggs was so determined to get me on his side if he has to answer to her. "The men Nero has been seen with have been connected to drug deals and weapons shipments into the city. You need to tell us what you know about it."

I give a shrug. "Absolutely nothing. Because your information is wrong."

"I think you're lying," Lydia says. "I think you know far more than this dumb blonde act you're putting on. Which means you know how deep you're in—and what liability you have for his crimes now."

She shoves a legal pad over to me, and a pen. "You have a chance to get out of this mess. Tell us everything you know. Write it down. Give us the information we need to charge Nero for his crimes—and protect yourself."

I pick up the pen, weighing it in my hand. I'm surprised to find it's a good one: black, with gold trim. There's an insignia on it, too, and I recognize the logo of the hotel where I met Greggs a few weeks ago.

"So, you're offering me immunity?" I ask, curious just how far they'll take this.

They exchange a look. "It depends on what you tell us," Greggs says. "How you can help link Nero to the delivery we picked up yesterday."

*Because they have no link.*

I put the pen down.

"You know, it's interesting," I muse sweetly. "You've clearly been sniffing around Nero and his business for months now, yet here you are, with absolutely nothing connecting him to any criminal activity. You wouldn't need me if you did. Well, I'm sorry to disappoint you."

"You're not going to cooperate." Lydia says flatly.

"Oh no, I'm happy to tell you what I know," I smile. Miles tenses beside me, but I don't stop. "Which is that I was with Nero all day. He didn't go near any warehouse—or talk to anyone who did."

## Ruthless Games

I don't hesitate. I don't drop my eyes. And I don't say another word.

I can see the surprise on their faces. Lydia looks pissed, and Greggs take the opportunity to take charge of the conversation.

"You know that if you're providing an alibi, you'll have to be willing to do so in a court of law. That's means that if you're lying to us right now, you're committing perjury. It's a serious crime, Lily."

I don't flinch. I'm stuck between a rock and a hard place right now. If Nero goes to jail? My protection is over. I'm as good as dead.

Lies are my only option.

"Shall we go now?" I ask Miles, getting to my feet.

"You're making a mistake here," Lydia scowls.

"No, the mistake is that hairstyle," I tell her, flashing a smile. "It makes your face look tired. Very aging, you know."

Miles scrambles to his feet, and follows me to the door, but Lydia blocks my path.

"We gave you a chance, but you've made your bed. Now, you have to lie in it."

"What's that?" I turn to Miles. "A threat?"

"Sure sounded like one," he says. "I'll add it to our harassment complaint. And you better believe, we expect Mr Barretti to be released now, without charge."

Lydia glares at me, "When we take him down—and we will - you're going right down with him."

I hide the shot of fear. "Bangs," I say instead. "I think bangs would really work on you. Soften everything up."

And then I walk out. But my heart pounds in fear, all the way out the building.

I just lied. Perjured myself like it was nothing—and waved a red flag in front of Agent Compton.

This plan better work.

# Chapter 11

## *Lily*

I wait in the lobby, while Miles goes to get Nero processed and released. My mind goes back over the interview, heart still racing with adrenaline and pride.

I can't believe I pulled it off.

But I know, my victory will be short-lived. Lydia Compton is a force to be reckoned with, and now she's gunning for the both of us. She reminds me of Nero in that way: Both determined individuals, with the kind of raw intensity that lets you know they'll do just about anything to get what they want.

You don't want to get in the way of a person like that... But that's exactly what I just did.

"It shouldn't be long now," Miles rejoins me, giving a weary sigh. He's been up all night too, by the looks of things, and his tie is crooked; his blonde hair ruffled out of place.

"So, is this your usual job description?" I ask, curious.

"Whatever it takes to protect the Barretti businesses," he says with a nod. "Nero put me through law school, he always said I would be wasted on the street. Can't throw a punch to save my life," he adds with a wry grin. "But file an emergency motion against extended custody proceedings? That's my kind of game."

I look at him again, surprised to hear he grew up in the organization. But maybe I shouldn't be. Nero likes to keep people close. "And you never thought about leaving? Taking a job someplace else."

He looks at me like I'm crazy. "I'm a Barretti," he says simply. "Not by blood, sure, but they're my family. I owe Nero everything, and I'm going to repay that debt."

Honor. Loyalty. Nero inspires it in almost everyone. It's no wonder his men didn't rat him out.

A pair of doors swing open, and then Nero walks out, still wearing his tuxedo from last night. The tie has been removed and he looks a mess, but my heart still turns over at the sight of him.

"Nero." I leap up, rushing to throw my arms around his neck.

He flinches back, anger radiating..

"Let's get the hell out of here," he says to Miles—looking straight past me like I'm not even here.

Is he serious?

My own anger rises as I follow them to the car and ride home. Nero doesn't say a word to me, and I bite my own tongue, until we're back at the house, and the door slams shut behind us.

We're finally alone.

"What the hell is your problem?" I demand, throwing my bag down on the floor.

"That's what I was going to ask you. They said I alibi-ed out for the raid. You told them I was with you all day. Lily, you *lied*."

I gape at him in disbelief. "And now you're mad at me? I did what I had to do to get you free!"

Nero scowls, his face dark with anger. "I never asked you to do that. In fact, I told you to stay the hell out."

"Then it's a good thing I have the ability to think for myself," I shoot back. "Otherwise, you'd still be in custody right now."

Nero rakes a hand through his hair, looking anguished. "But why, Lily? You just put yourself directly in the firing line. Why did you do that?"

"Because you're my husband!"

My voice echoes, and then there's silence. I see Nero's expression shift from anger to something more passionate. Emotion flaring in his eyes.

He strides across the room and pulls me into his arms. Kissing me wildly, passionately, like a man possessed. I cling to him, already tearing at his shirt. I need him inside me.

"No." he growls, pulling back. "Not here. This time, I'm taking you to my bed."

He scoops me in his arms as if I weigh nothing and carries me upstairs—straight to the room he's been sleeping in. The primary suite. He keeps walking, into the bathroom.

"I stink of jail," he growls, depositing me on the counter, and turning on the shower spray.

"I don't care," I moan, reaching for him, but he steps back. Stripping off his clothes until he's naked.

"I do. I told you, baby. You don't belong in the dirt."

He steps into the shower, lathering up as the steam billows. I watch for a moment, reveling in the sight of him: his hard muscles, the mysterious tattoos...

All mine.

I climb down, and slip out of my clothes, joining him in the huge shower stall. I snake my arms around him, soaping him up, letting my hands trail over every inch of him.

Nero groans.

"I missed you," I whisper, kissing his naked back. "I had to spend the whole night without you. You haven't been inside me for *days*."

Nero spins around, pinning me back against the tiled wall. "Dammit, baby. You've got a filthy mouth."

"You love it," I whisper, arching up, slick and naked against him.

"Fuck yeah, I do."

Nero runs his hands down my sides, tracing my curves. My body is a live wire, aching for his touch. When he bends his head to lick over my breasts, I shudder in pleasure, pressing closer to the thick, stiff ridge between us. I wrap my hand around his cock and start to pump.

He bucks against me, groaning as he sucks wetly on one nipple. "Fuck, that feels so good," he says, voice growing labored. "Tighter baby, warm me up for your cunt."

I moan, gripping harder. His hand slips between my legs, and finds my slick core, rubbing at my clit and delving his fingers into my wetness. Our eyes lock, and for a moment, we're suspended there under the water, matching each other stroke for stroke, breath for breath, barreling to the edge of chaos.

Then Nero grips my waist, lifting me, pinning me back against the wall. "Wider, baby," he growls, as I spread my legs to allow him access, wrapping them around his waist. "Let me all the way in."

He finds my entrance, and sinks in deep, stretching me out around his thick, weighty cock.

*Fuck.*

I throw back my head and groan from the sweet intrusion,

the friction adding to the inferno building inside. "*Yes*, Nero, God yes."

He grinds up into me, holding me there, impaled on his dick. "So goddamn tight. Baby, your pussy doesn't want to let me go."

"So don't go," I gasp, struggling for purchase. I grip his shoulders, and thrust against him, raising and lowering myself on his cock. "Stay right here, where you belong."

Nero lets out a ragged curse at that. His eyes flash with passion, as he withdraws, then pistons into me again. "Not going anywhere," he vows, fucking me deeper. "Going to give this pussy everything she deserves."

I let out a strangled cry of pleasure as he pulls back and drives forward again, finding an incredible rhythm that sends me wild with every stroke. He's so strong, lifting me up, holding me in place, and that's almost as much of a turn-on as the look in his eyes, the one that tells me he's just as crazy as I am. The pleasure is overwhelming.

I'm already teetering at the edge of ecstasy.

"Oh God," I cry out, my heart hammering so hard that I swear I can hear it echoing in my ears. "Nero... I'm going to... Gonna..."

"Do it," he growls out between clenched teeth. "Drip that sugar all over my cock. Show me how you need it."

His dirty words seal the deal, and my orgasm shatters me. I buck against him, and his hands tighten on my ass. He'll probably leave bruises, but I don't care. It'll be a reminder of this, the perfection of the moment as he finds his own release. His cock leaps inside of me, and he buries his face in my neck, nipping the skin there as he lets out an animal groan, shuddering in my arms.

As we both come back down to earth, I know that our fates

are completely intertwined now. I've made my choice, and it's him.

Maybe I'm crazy, but I can't go back now. This flame will consume me.

And I can't get enough.

## Chapter 12

### *Lily*

We dry off and fall into bed together, making up for lost time. Exploring each other's bodies and ignoring the incessant buzz of Nero's cellphone inside his pants on the floor. It's early afternoon, and we're not dressed, but I don't care. I'm more at ease right now than I've felt in a long time.

Nothing has really changed, except that I've finally decided what side I'm on in all this. I'm not just along for the ride, trying to decide if I'm going to talk to the FBI or not. I've firmly aligned myself with Nero, and while that's scary, because of the dangerous lifestyle he lives, it's also somehow freeing. I'm not stuck in that dark, uncertain place anymore, afraid to make a decision and unsure about what's right.

I'm following my heart. And it's always led me straight back to him.

"When did you get this one?" I ask, tracing the tribal-style band tattooed around his bicep. It's comprised of thick black lines intersecting and completely encompasses his arm. "It must have hurt when the artist did your inner arm."

"Like a bitch," he admits with a grin. "But don't tell anyone that. I just got it last year."

The two of us are laying on our sides, facing each other, with the sheets barely slung over our naked bodies. It's the first time I've had the luxury of reveling in the afterglow with him, sunlight streaming through the windows, and the outside world the last thing on our minds.

"And this one?" I lightly brush my fingers over his pectoral muscle, where the skull is.

"That one's much older. Eight years." He pauses, a shadow passing over his expression. "Some things need to be remembered, you know?"

I nod, but I don't press. I don't need to hear what dark occasion he was marking. It's all in the past.

My fingertips move onwards, tracing the rest of his ink, and the smooth planes of his muscles. "I've thought about getting one," I muse, stretching. "Maybe something small and girly on my hip, like a butterfly or a rose."

"If you get a flower, it should be a lily," he says, tracing the spot on my hipbone. He leans down and presses his lips there, making me giggle. His hands trail warmly over my thighs, languid, like we have all the time in the world.

I sigh happily. I like him like this. He's so relaxed, and the casual touches make my heart flutter every time. The stern, tortured man I married is nowhere to be seen, and in his place is a glimpse of the boy I once knew. The one who won my heart.

It's touching to know that he's not gone forever.

"Let's get away."

Nero lifts his head, a playful smile on his face.

"What?" I blink, shocked. "Now?"

"Why not?" he grins. " I never gave you a proper honeymoon, so let's go somewhere right now. Get all romantic, away from everything."

"Is that even possible?" I ask, my excitement growing. "With everything happening right now..."

"Even more reason to get some distance." Nero sits up, pushing back his messy dark hair. "What do you say? The Feds would probably take it the wrong way if I left the country, but we could do something here. How about San Francisco?" he suggests. "Have you ever been?"

"I... No. I mean, yes, that sounds amazing." I can't believe it. It's so spontaneous and thoughtful, I never would have expected this from him in a million years.

"Then let's do it." Nero leans over and kisses me. "Next stop: California."

\* \* \*

Just a few hours later, we're clear across the country. I should have guessed Nero would barely blink at the logistics: From the first-class flight to the fancy rental car to the luxurious hotel room, everything has just appeared out of nowhere.

The man knows how to get what he wants.

"After you," he says, smiling, as he ushers me into the hotel lobby. It's huge and glamorous, with deco details and an old school charm. Thanks to the time difference, it's still afternoon, and it's a clear, sunny day.

A concierge meets us right there. "Mr. Barretti, I hope you had a pleasant flight. Please, allow me to show you to your suite."

He leads us straight to the elevator, bypassing the line of guests at the check-in desk.

I smile. "The last trip I took, I drove with a girlfriend to Albuquerque," I note wryly, smiling as we step into the gilded elevator. "We lived off vending machine junk food and slept in a crummy motel by the freeway. This is quite the upgrade."

Nero smiles, arm slung around my shoulder. "Nothing but the best for my baby."

And he means it. Our room is the penthouse suite on the top floor, with incredible views of the city. I can even see the Golden Gate Bridge in the distance. It's beautiful.

"Are you hungry?" Nero asks, as the concierge leaves us alone. Our bags have already been set by the door, and there's a luxurious bedroom just off the living area, with a canopied four-poster bed.

His arms wrap around me from behind, and I smile, snuggling back against him. "Depends what for…" I tease, and he rumbles with a laugh. His hands skim lower, suggestive, but I pull away. We could easily spend all weekend in bed, but I'm itching to get out and explore. "What do you want to see first?" I ask, reaching for the tourist guides stacked on the bureau. "We could go to Fisherman's Wharf, or the Trocadero, or just walk around…"

"I have a couple of ideas." Nero gives a mysterious smile. "Have you heard of a museum called The Legion of Honor?"

"Are you kidding?" I exclaim. "They have an amazing collection of Rodin sculptures. The biggest outside France."

"I figured, since I can't take you to Paris just yet, Paris will just have to come to us."

I trade jackets, and grab my purse, and I'm all set to go. We head back down to the lobby, and as Nero guides me out of the door, he nestles his hand on the small of my back. I notice that he's doing that more and more, little public displays of affection that make my heart sing, and by the time we reach the museum, his hand is intertwined in mine.

I look around. The museum is set on a clifftop, overlooking

the bay, with an incredible sculpture garden and all kinds of amazing exhibitions.

"Where first?" Nero asks. "You're the expert."

"I don't know where to begin!" I laugh, overwhelmed with the choices. For an art lover, this is just about heaven.

"How about we start here, and work our way around?" he suggests, nodding to the nearest room.

"Sounds like a plan!"

We take our time, strolling among the exhibits, and it doesn't take long before I'm swept up in the beauty of the art around us. At first, I'm worried that Nero will be bored, but he seems happy to listen as I pour over the guide booklet and linger by my favorite works. I spend a long time in the Hall of Antiquities, checking out ancient works from Egypt, Greece, and Rome. But it's the collection of European art that really blows me away. Much of it is from France, which is why they have such a large Rodin collection. But there's more than sculpture. As much as I enjoy the three-dimensional art, I'm drawn to the paintings above all else.

I can only hope to someday create such amazing pieces that are worthy of hanging in a museum. Nero is silent beside me, and I can't stop giving him sidelong glances out of the corner of my eye. He seems to be just as interested in the artwork as I am, and his hand is warm against mine.

The museum is busy with tourists and other visitors, and it's easy to pretend we're just like them: No drama, no mafia threats, no FBI on our trail, just a pair of ordinary newlyweds, taking in the sights.

In my fantasy, the only potential problems in our new marriage are little things, like disagreements about where to go for dinner or what color to paint the bedroom. Prison, death, blood feuds... They couldn't be more far away.

It's a nice fantasy, and I wish it could last forever, but eventually, Nero glances at his phone.

"I should really check in," he says, sounding apologetic. "Make sure Chase hasn't burned the place down in my absence."

I nod. "Take your time," I tell him, not worried. After all, we're on the other side of the country, and whatever is going down in New York couldn't be more far away. "I have plenty to look at!"

"I'll be right back."

Nero heads outside to make his call, and I continue to browse the displays. It's truly absorbing here, and I'm not sure how much time passes before I realize that Nero has been gone for a long time. I figure he's lost track of me in the rabbit-warren hallways, so I retrace my steps, and head outside in the direction I saw him last.

And then I spot him, half-hidden deep in the sculpture garden, talking to an older man I've never seen before.

But it's clear, the two of them know each other. Reading their body language, I can tell this isn't a casual conversation. Nero is frowning, focused and alert, and while his body is facing the stranger, he's kept enough space between them to tell me that he doesn't fully trust the guy.

Something's going on. Something serious.

But how the hell did anyone find us here, of all places?

Unless...

This was Nero's plan all along. His reason for this romantic getaway—not to spend time with me, but to stage this secret meeting, away from the prying eyes of the FBI back in New York.

I just stand there, simmering with rage as I watch Nero talk, his expression stern. I'm not going to let this go. He's up to something, despite telling me that this trip was for us. For *me*.

Finally, the two of them part with a handshake. The man passes me, heading back inside, and gives me a brief nod as he goes. Then Nero sees me. He looks startled for a second before his face goes stoic and he walks over.

I fold my arms. The easy happiness I felt before is gone now. The outside world is back, with all its drama and betrayal.

"So," I say, not bothering to hide my anger. "Do you want to tell me why we're really here?"

# Chapter 13

## *Lily*

There's a heavy moment of silence as Nero just stares as me. I have a feeling that he's choosing his words very carefully.

"We're here for a fun getaway," he finally says.

I laugh, but there's no humor in it. "Oh right. Our delayed honeymoon."

He doesn't even crack a smile.

"Yes. And... I'm taking care of some business while we're here in town."

"I knew it," I snap. I turn away from him, finding that I suddenly don't even want the details anymore. I'm too hurt to listen to another word.

I head around the side of the building, making for the main exit with tears stinging in the corner of my eyes. But Nero's hot on my heels. He grabs my arm, spinning me around to face him.

"Let's talk about this."

"No." I shake my head. "There's nothing to say. You lied to me, made me believe that we could have something *normal*.

Just one little weekend for us, it shouldn't be asking too much. But surprise, surprise, it is."

Nero looks stubborn. "I wouldn't be here if it wasn't important."

"You mean, spending time with me isn't?" I throw back at him.

He winces. "You know what I mean."

"I know that Barretti business always comes first."

"Can you blame me?" Nero explodes. "That Barretti business could get you killed or locked up for life. So yes, right now it is more important than our honeymoon. I don't care about a weekend together, when what matters is the rest of our lives!"

I sigh, hating the fact he's making sense. No matter how much I want to pretend the real world isn't waiting for us, that would be naïve.

"So tell me then," I say, still mad, despite everything. "Who was that guy?"

Nero exhales. "I'm trying to organize a meeting with the head of the Kovak gang. Man-to-man, no bullshit. We can't go on like this, losing men, sabotaging each other. It has to end."

"How?" I ask, feeling a chill.

"I don't know yet. It's not going to be easy, but I'm going to negotiate a cease-fire."

"Alone?" my voice rises again. "How can you be sure you can trust them? They could come for you, right here in San Francisco. You don't have any muscle backing you up."

I look around, fearful. In New York, we had Barretti men guarding our every move. But here?

We're exposed.

"It's a parlay," Nero says. "They'll honor the terms."

"Honor. From organized crime. Sure." My sarcasm is thick, hiding my fear.

Nero scowls. "I'll do what it takes," he says, and my anger bubbles up again.

"So when's this sit-down happening?" I demand.

"Soon." Nero checks his phone. "You should head back to the hotel. And stay there."

"And what, I'm supposed to just wait for you?"

"Yes." Nero takes my hand. "Trust me on this, Lily. I'm sorry I lied to you," he says, gazing into my eyes. "But I had to take the chance to meet, away from the city, where nobody can know. It might be my only shot to secure our future."

I soften. "Be safe, OK?" I say, swallowing hard.

He nods. "You too."

Back at the hotel, I wait, my nerves growing more anxious with every passing minute. I try to distract myself, ordering room service, and watching TV on the expensive flatscreen, but nothing can distract me from the danger Nero might be in, right at this second.

As my anger has cooled, I'm left feeling hurt and worried, running over worst-case scenarios in my mind.

What if Nero is wrong about this meeting? Everyone says, the Kovaks are a ruthless, brutal gang. If these are his enemies, this could be an ambush. They could take the chance to cut the head off the entire Barretti operation in one fell swoop.

I pace the length of our hotel suite, full of restless energy. I hate that Nero is doing this, that he tricked me into coming here for his mafia ploy, but I'm also terrified that he won't return.

I should've stopped him from going. I was so upset, that I wasn't thinking clearly.

I didn't even tell him that I love him.

And now it might be too late.

I want to see where this marriage is going, but that'll never happen if he doesn't return.

When the lock on the hotel room door clicks and it starts to open, I rush over with my heart in my throat. I put the chain on for safety, so the door only opens a few inches before stopping, but I can see Nero through the gap.

I've never been so happy to see his gorgeous, brooding face.

"It's me," he says, and I can't tell from his voice whether the meeting was a success.

"Oh, thank God." I let him in, grabbing him in a big hug. I hold him close, feeling his heart beating, and his arms going around me, safe and secure. "I was so worried. What happened?"

I finally pull back so I can look at him again. "How did it go? What did they say?"

Nero crosses to the room bar and pours himself a drink. He knocks it back in one, and then pours again, while I wait, anxious.

"I think... I think they'll take the deal," he says, and I exhale in relief.

"You mean, a truce?"

"More than that." Nero nods, swirling the booze around his glass. "A buyout. The plan is, to hand over territory, cede our control over certain parts of the operation to the Kovaks."

My eyes go wide. I wasn't expecting that.

"I don't understand." I say. "Why would you do that?"

"Because this has been my plan all along." Nero announces with a twisted smile. "Get out of this fucked up game and take the Barretti organization legit. The drugs, the protection rackets, it's petty shit. Old news. Nothing compared with the money we could be making through legal channels now."

"The real estate development," I say, realization finally dawning. It's been Nero's number one priority since I arrived.

Hell, it's the reason he cut a deal to protect me in the first place: Get him McKenna's vote and get him the zoning approval for his project.

I thought it was just about the money, but now I see, it's more than that.

It's his big play for the future. *Our* future.

"You really want to quit that stuff?" I ask, half-disbelieving. "The Barretti empire is built on it."

He nods. "And the fucking foundations are crumbling more every year. It's not like when my father was coming up. Shit's gone high-tech. Not just our side, but the Feds, too. They have computer surveillance, AI, all the banks running scared. And meanwhile, we're all still stuck playing by the old rules, spilling blood on street corners, and for what? It's not worth it," he says, with a frustrated shrug. "Not when the real money is right there for the taking, and we don't have to break a single law."

"Well, almost," I give him a knowing grin. "Blackmail and extortion aren't exactly legal."

He chuckles. "Old habits die hard."

I take it all in. It must have taken years of planning, and I look at Nero with a new admiration, seeing how he's waited patiently, step by step, lining up every part of this to make the pieces fit.

"So, the Kovaks will buy up the dirty business?" I ask, moving to the couch. Nero takes a seat beside me, relaxing back with a nod.

"I'm essentially selling off the criminal side of our enterprise. Trade routes, suppliers, the whole lot of it. Which will cause a whole lot of shit when they hear about it in New York."

"They don't matter." I stretch my legs out, draping them across his lap. "It's your empire now. You get to call the shots."

I pause, something else occurring to me. "It would mean less risk from the FBI, wouldn't it?" I ask. "If you give up the criminal parts of the organization to the Kovaks, they can't come after you anymore."

"They might try and dredge up the past, but yeah, our liability goes way down. We'd be legit," Nero says. "Focus on real estate, and the genuine businesses. Not hiding in the shadows anymore."

"Are you sure about this?" I ask, not because I think it's a bad idea, but because it's huge. He's taking a big chance here.

"All the way. It would change everything for us." Nero takes my hand. "We would be safe."

My heart is racing. "It sounds too good to be true." I whisper.

"That's because it is," he replies. "It's not a done deal, not yet. There's going to be resistance on both sides, to put it mildly. And a bargain like this requires trust, not something that's easy to come by in this business. But I have to try," he adds, eyes full of determination. "It's the only way we'll have a future. Not just my crew, but us. You and me."

I feel a wave of emotion surge through me. I reach for him, and Nero meets me halfway, claiming my mouth in a slow, devastating kiss.

"You'd do this for us?" I echo, pressing closer.

"Anything," he growls.

He lays me back on the couch, kissing me again as he pins my wrists above my head with one hand.

I shiver in anticipation, my body already reacting to his dominant gesture. "What are you—"

"Shh," Nero places his finger to my lips. "I'm done talking. And you're done asking questions."

A small part of me wants to challenge him, just to see what'll happen, but I'm too breathless. The look on his face is tantalizing, the way his gaze moves over my body like he owns it.

## Ruthless Games

The hungry expression in his eyes.

"Don't move," he orders me, as he releases my wrists.

"Or what?" I ask, wriggling in anticipation.

He silences me with a look. "Or I'll take you over my knee and spank the disobedience out of you."

I suck in a breath, my pulse kicking. *Oh my god.* I'm tempted to test his sexy promise, but I force myself to hold still, laying there with my hands above my head.

He has something in mind for tonight, and I want to find out.

Nero stands, holding my eyes as he starts to slowly undress.

It's amazing how hard it is to hold my position as I watch, my core flooding with heat at the sight of his sculpted body. The dips and curves of his muscles are what fantasies are made of.

God knows I've thought about him in the dark of night over the last ten years, dreaming of the way he could touch me. Pleasure me. Fuck me into submission.

And now, he's mine.

Nero strips down to his briefs, and then returns to me, his erection jutting out under the fabric, making my mouth water for a taste. His hands go to my shirt, stripping it over my head. My bra is lace with a front clasp, which Nero makes quick work of flicking open.

"Look at you," he murmurs, trailing a hand over my bared breasts. "All laid out for me like a present. I don't even know where to start."

He pinches my nipple, making it sting, but just as quickly, his head dips, tongue lavishing the pain. I sigh, relaxing as he blows lightly over the sensitive peaks, making them stiffen with sensation.

I arch eagerly against his mouth, needing more, but he places a hand on my chest and pushes me back into the couch.

"I told you, don't move."

I shiver at the steel in his voice. There's something powerful and commanding about him: Nero the boss, controlling everything in his domain.

Including me.

I let my legs fall open, inviting him. Nero smirks. "Impatient, hmm? Just for that, I'm going to make you wait."

As if to prove his point, he trails his lips down my stomach. My core clenches tight in anticipation. But he doesn't remove my skirt right away. Instead, he peppers kisses along my waistband, the ultimate tease.

His hands caress me, and I start to tremble, the sensation rolling through me, irresistible. It's so good and we've barely gotten started.

He inches my skirt higher, fingertips light on my skin, and I whimper.

"Is this sweet pussy getting wet for me?" Nero muses, taking his sweet time exploring my inner thighs.

"Yes," I gasp, clutching the cushions. *"Please."*

He gives a low, dangerous chuckle, fingertips barely brushing over my damp panties. "Begging is useless, baby. You know, I won't touch you until I'm damn well ready."

*Fuck.* I've never been with a man that was this good at bringing me pleasure. With just light kisses and his fingers skimming over me, he's winding me up tight. I want to explode already, but he knows what he's doing. He barely brushes over my clit, backing off as soon as I start moaning, drawing out the pleasure until it's driving me crazy.

His fingers slide under my panties and dip into my entrance, just another tease at first, but then, he's got two of them moving in and out while his thumb stays pressed against my clit.

*Oh god.* I'm panting, and I still haven't moved my hands.

He's kneeling beside me, and all I want to do is touch that big cock of his, to drive him crazy like he's doing to me until he can't take anymore and fucks me senseless.

But the torture of denying myself is all a part of heightening my pleasure. There's no breaking him when he's like this.

But damn, I want to try.

I reach for him, stroking his erection through the fabric of his briefs. I need to touch him so badly, to take some of the control back.

And maybe I want to test him.

His hand catches my wrist before I can stroke his swollen cock. "What did I tell you?" he says sternly. He pins my hands to the couch again, this time more forcefully. I try to get loose, but he's too strong, even with just one hand.

"Play with fire baby... And you're going to get burned."

He moves his other hand down my body, pinching my nipple hard enough to make my eyes water. I gasp, bucking against him, but he's immoveable. His lips capture mine, and he takes my lower lip into his mouth, nipping it. It stings, but he soothes it right away by running his tongue over the area.

The message is clear.

*Don't disobey.*

"Don't make me spank you," he growls, "because I won't stop until that hot little ass of yours is bright red."

That's shouldn't turn me on as much as it does... And he notices.

"You'd like that, baby?" His hand moves to my pussy, testing my wetness. I moan. "Yeah, I think you would. Getting punished like a bad girl, until you're all messed up and sticky for me."

He grabs my hip, flipping my body over so I'm facedown on the couch with my hands sill pinned above my head. Nero yanks my skirt off, and my panties down.

"Ass up, baby. You asked for it."

The first slap still takes me by surprise, sharp and stinging on my naked behind. I let out a little yelp, and Nero answers with a satisfied growl.

"See, baby? I'm not playing. You push me, and I *will* give you exactly what you deserve, every damn time."

He spanks me again, but this time, I'm ready. The shock of sensation jolts through me, and I gasp, my blood running hotter. I've never felt anything like this before.

A moan falls from my lips.

"Fuck princess, listen to yourself." Nero curses. "My bad girl wants me to spank all the sass right out of her."

He spanks me again, harder, until tears sting in the corners of my eyes and I'm gasping for air. But the pain is laced with pleasure, and soon, he's rubbing my ass with soothing, tender strokes.

And then moving lower. His fingers expertly find my clit, rubbing in tight little circles that don't stop, won't stop—

I climax suddenly in a rush of pleasure.

*Fuck!*

My orgasm rips through me. I bury my face in the cushions and scream.

"That's it, baby," Nero's voice is thick with satisfaction. "Your body belongs to me. And I know exactly what it needs, every fucking time."

I gasp for air, as he picks up my limp body, and strides to the bedroom, dropping me on the massive bed with a bounce.

I shudder, gazing up at him, pleasure still coursing in my veins. He looms over me as I lay there naked.

I open my arms to him. My legs. Inviting him in.

But still, Nero holds back. "My rules tonight," he growls. "You may drive me crazy not listening to a damn word I say out there in the world, but here?"

He strokes over my body, still quivering from my orgasm. I gasp.

"Yeah, here, you love obeying me, don't you? It makes that tight cunt of yours clench harder, every time I tell you what to do."

"Yes," I moan, my desire burning up inside me. "Nero, please. Tell me what you want. I'll do it, I swear."

"Then come over here and suck my cock." Nero strips off his briefs, standing by the edge of the bed. His erection rears up, thick and hard, and I eagerly scoot closer on my knees, to encircle him with my hands and lick up the long, straining shaft.

He groans, tangling his hands in my hair to take control, immediately thrusting into my mouth in a sharp, deep rhythm. "That's it. Just like that, baby. Every fucking inch."

I angle my head, feeling a rush of pride at his ragged tone as I take him deeper. I love to pleasure him, the way it makes me feel to drive *him* to the brink. Hollowing my cheeks, I bob up and down, swirling my tongue over him, lost in a haze of surrender and desire.

"Maybe I'll come just like this," Nero muses, tilting my head up to look at him as he slowly thrusts into my mouth. "Spill down your tight little throat, leave you all worked up and panting as punishment."

I whimper in protest, and he smiles, gently cupping my cheek. It's a tender gesture that contrasts with the way he's fucking my mouth, so deep I almost gag.

"But you're taking me so good, you deserve a reward. And nothing feels as good as that tight pussy going off around my cock."

*Yes!*

He pulls out, moving me back on the bed, covering my body with his weight. I moan, wrapping my arms around his neck, eagerly arching to meet him with my thighs spread wide as I feel his thick head nudge at my entrance.

He pauses there, looking down at me with dark, flashing eyes.

"You need this, baby?" he asks, already knowing the answer. It has to be written on my face at this point, and my pussy is getting wetter and wetter, preparing for what I need so badly.

"Yes," I moan, as he nudges again, sinking just an inch inside. Fuck, I want it more than anything.

"Look at you, trying to grab it all." he sinks in another inch, so slowly, I think I'm going to lose my mind. "This greedy pussy needs my cock."

"Please," I whimper, trying to thrust against him. But Nero has me pinned down, I can't hurry him, and all I can do is take it.

Inch by devastating inch.

"*Fuck.*" Nero's eyes go glassy as he moves a little deeper inside me. "So goddamn tight."

"Nero," I cry, struggling against his hold. "I need it. Fuck me. *Please.*"

"Why? You going to come like this?" Nero growls, motionless above me. "Get off on just a couple of inches, because even that's better than any man you've ever had?"

"Yes!" I gasp, heat rising. "Fuck, Nero..."

The sensation of being trapped, totally surrendered to him, is getting me so worked up I can barely breathe. I can't believe it, but my orgasm is already building, just from his denial, and the shallow intrusion, his thick girth still barely sinking inside me.

"Fuck baby, you're a miracle." Nero groans. "I could make you beg all goddamn night, but I can't. Because it feels too goddamn good!"

With a roar, he thrusts all the way in, burying his cock to the hilt.

I shatter right away. "Nero!" I scream, another orgasm ripping through me, stronger this time. Sweeter. I shudder around him in a frenzy, but he doesn't even pause for air.

He fucks me into the mattress like there's no tomorrow.

"This is what you wanted," he growls, slamming into me so hard I see stars. I scream, my orgasm still ricocheting, driving me to higher planes of pleasure. "Every fucking inch. So take it, princess. Take it all!"

I claw at him, mindless, sobbing as he drives into me, over and over. It's a whirlwind, a hurricane, my body has no choice but to submit to every brutal thrust until I'm screaming his name like a prayer, loud enough for the whole city to hear. I lose track of where one climax ends and the next begins, until finally, Nero unleashes a powerful roar, rearing up inside me, spurting hot and deep as we fall over the edge of chaos and into the black.

And I know I'll never be the same. Because now I know what it's like to surrender so completely to him...

Nothing will ever feel this good again.

# Chapter 14

## *Lily*

When I wake up in the morning, my body is sore... in the best possible way.

Rolling over in bed, I stretch with my arms above my head and let out a huge, satisfied yawn. I can hear Nero is in the shower nearby, and I revel in the moment alone to process everything that happened last night.

*Oh my god.*

I want to laugh in delight. I never knew sex could be like that. So intense. So mind-blowingly hot. The trust that's building between Nero and me is translating to the most incredible orgasms of my life. If someone had asked me a month ago if I would have surrendered to him like that, I would have laughed and called them crazy. But now not only did I do it willingly, but it's the most incredible feeling in the world.

I sit up in bed, reaching for the room service menu. We worked up an appetite, and I'm going to need my fuel if we're going to do that again.

And I definitely want a repeat performance.

I'm trying to decide between eggs and pancakes when my phone rings on the nightstand.

"Hello?" I answer, still distracted.

"Hi, is this Lily?"

It's a male voice, youngish. I pause, waking up properly. "Who is this?" I demand.

"My name's Dustin. I'm Teddy's roommate."

My stomach drops. I can't think of a single reason that my brother's roommate would call unless it's bad news. Panic grips me in the space of five seconds.

"Is something wrong? Where's Teddy?"

"Well, that's the thing." He replies, sounding reluctant. "I don't really know. I was hoping that maybe you'd heard from him recently?"

"You don't know? What's that mean?"

My voice is getting higher with each frantic question. I leap out of the bed, heart pounding with panic.

"It's probably nothing, just... I haven't seen him since Thursday. I figured it was a late night thing, but I just came back to the room and his bed hasn't been slept in again."

Thursday. It's Saturday morning now. Which means... "He's been gone for two days?!"

"Listen, I have to get to practice," Dustin sounds hurried. "It's probably nothing. Just tell him to give me a buzz if you hear from him. K?"

He hangs up, leaving me standing naked in the middle of a hotel room, panic blaring through my system.

Teddy is gone. Something terrible has happened.

Worst-case scenarios flash through my mind. The Kovak gang. Rogue Barretti men. Feds. Or just the random violence that happens in this country every day.

*My baby brother.*

I immediately call his cellphone, but the phone just goes straight to voicemail.

"If you're getting this message, I'm out being awesome. Catch you later!"

"Teddy? It's Lily. Call me the *minute* you get this."

I lower the phone, reeling. I need to do something, but what? I cross to my suitcase, and start pulling on clothes. My mind is consumed with fear. Teddy is my reason for everything. I've been fighting for his safety more than even my own. He's the last hope for my family, really. He's untouched by all this mafia drama and darkness. Even after we ran into Witness Protection, he was shielded from the worst of it, young enough to start over like nothing had happened.

He has a chance for a normal, happy life. And I want that for him more than anything.

I *need* him to be okay.

Nero steps out of the bathroom with a towel wrapped around his waist. "What's going on?" he asks, confused, as I throw things in my case, shaking.

"Teddy's gone."

Just saying the words makes bile rise in the back of my throat.

"What?" Nero crosses the room to me.

"His roommate called me." I gulp. "He hasn't been back to his dorm for... They don't know. A day? Two? I can't reach him. He's...He's *gone*."

"Fuck." Nero immediately begins pulling on his clothes.

I pause, watching. A terrible thought taking hold.

"You didn't... I mean, your guys didn't take him, did they?"

"Are you serious?" he asks, turning to stare at me.

I would swear that he seems almost offended right now, but how can he? He's held the threat of killing me and my brother over my head too many times to act like I'm out of line with my question.

"I need to know." I demand, freaking out. "He's a loose end. You wanted him in custody, didn't you?"

"No. Lily. No." Nero grips me by the arms. "You need to take a deep breath. I'm sure he's fine."

"Are you?" I shoot back. "Can you look at me, and swear on your life that he's safe right now? That nobody's got to him as a way of striking you?"

Nero's eyes flash. He doesn't reply.

"Exactly." I tear away. "I swear to God, if he's hurt because of you, I will never forgive you. *Never*, do you hear me?"

Sobs well up, I can't even think of it.

"Shhh," Nero comforts me, his arms strong and safe around me. "We'll find him."

I want to believe him. Still, I pull away, trying to think straight. "We should call the cops in Indiana. The university, too."

Nero shakes his head. "No cops."

I whirl on him. "This is my *brother!*"

"And cops will only make it more complicated," he insists. "Do you want Teddy getting dragged into all of this? Flagged for the FBI?"

I pause. "But we have to do something."

"And we will. Right now." Nero promises. "We'll go, and we'll track him down. I swear to you, Lily. I'll find him, no matter what."

I exhale, shaky. I have no choice right now.

I have to trust him.

"OK."

Nero gives a tight nod and pulls out his phone. "Let's go."

· · ·

Somehow, Nero organizes a private jet to take us straight to an airfield near the college campus. Any other time, I would be luxuriating in the privacy and swanky surroundings, but the whole trip is a blur. All I can think about is what might have happened to Teddy; terrible scenarios flashing in my mind until I'm sick to my stomach.

He has to be OK.

I keep in touch with Dustin the whole time, probably driving him crazy with my constant text messages asking about updates on Teddy. But there is no update. By the time we arrive at the dorm, there's still been no sign of him.

"I've asked around," Dustin says, apologetically, showing us into their room. "But he's off the grid. Missed a study session, and we were going to throw a frisbee around this morning, too."

Dustin is short, around my height, with black hair in tight curls and a dimple in his cheek. He's so young, practically a kid, and Teddy is the same. He's innocent and stepping into the room really drives that point home for me. Teddy's bed is unmade, and there's a haphazard pile of comic books on the desk. He's hung up a poster from some recent superhero movie next to his bed.

It's exactly what I imagined, and that makes my heart hurt.

"Tell us about the last time you saw Teddy." Nero switches into action, cool and level-headed while I'm falling apart.

"Uhh..." Dustin looks nervous. I can't blame him. Nero looks serious as hell, and I feel an unexpected rush of appreciation for him at this moment.

"We went to a party at a fraternity two nights ago—" Dustin starts.

"Teddy's joining a fraternity?" I interrupt, surprised.

"No, that's not really our style. But the parties are fun. You know, for the girls." Dustin blushes.

"What happened at the party?" Nero presses, getting back on track.

"Nothing much." Dustin shrugs. "I hooked up with a freshman chick who turned out to be way too clingy, and I haven't seen Teddy since."

"You didn't see him leave the party?" Nero demands. "He hasn't checked in with you even once?"

"No." Dustin looks impatient. "I already told her this."

"And now you're telling me." Nero looms. "You guys are friends, right? Do you have any idea where he could have gone? A mutual friend's house? Did you check with anyone?"

"Yeah," Dustin protests. "I mean, I texted a couple of people..."

"Call everyone. Now."

Nero's tone of voice makes it clear that he isn't making a suggestion, and Dustin does as he says. I go to Teddy's desk, rifling through his textbooks and school papers, futilely looking for some clue.

My hands are shaking.

Suddenly, Nero is bedside me, reaching out and taking my hands in his. I turn to look at him, and the stark fear I feel must show on my face because there's sympathy in his eyes.

"I'll find him. Don't worry."

I almost want to laugh at those words. Not worrying is completely impossible right now.

But the fact that Nero is trying to help means something. It provides comfort in a way that nothing else could.

"Give me your phone," he says.

"What? Why."

"I need his number. I know a guy, we can track his phone," Nero says. "If someone's got him..." he looks grim. "I'll deal with them."

I hand it over immediately. "If he calls..."

"I'll come get you." Nero promises. He steps into the hallway, and places a call, talking in a low voice.

I pace, still jittery. For the first time, I'm glad for Nero's shady criminal contacts. If anyone can find Teddy, he will.

But what state will my brother be in?

I feel nauseous. He could be out there, hurt right now, needing my help. Bleeding by the side of the street somewhere. Even dead.

*No.*

I can't think of it, I'll go crazy like this. But I don't know what else to do. I've never felt so powerless in my life before. All this time, everything I've done, it's to keep Teddy safe. So that he could have the life I never did.

But what if my choices have put his life at risk?

I'm married to Nero now. A Barretti. Which means Teddy is linked to him too, whether he knows about it or not. And if the Kovaks were willing to hurt me to send a message to Nero, they wouldn't hesitate to strike at Teddy, either.

*I did this. I put him in danger.*

Just as I'm spiraling even deeper into despair, someone saunters down the hall. My breath catches in my throat as Teddy walks into the room. Perfectly unharmed, in jeans and a wrinkled T-shirt, with a paper coffee cup in his hand.

"Woah." He looks around, taking in our panicked faces. "Who died?"

With a sob, I launch myself into his arms.

## Chapter 15

### *Nero*

Thank *fuck.* Watching Lily sobbing in her brother's arms, I realize just how close I was to burning my whole world down: Ordering my guys to tear the Kovaks apart, truce be damned, just to see him safe again.

He's her family—which means he's mine, too. And there's nothing I won't do to keep my family safe.

"Where have you been?" Lily wails, finally releasing him. But her hands stay on his arms, clinging to them as if she's afraid he might disappear again.

"Around," Teddy looks baffled. Then he notices me and goes tense. He was just a kid before, but I can tell, he recognizes me. "Lily, what's going on? Why is *he* here?"

Lily swallows. "Don't duck the question," she says, thumping his arm. "Do you realize how worried we've all been? You were gone for two days!"

Teddy turns to his roommate. "You ratted me out to my sister?"

"I just figured she might've heard from you," Dustin says, wincing.

"We called." Lily continues, her relief giving way to anger. "And texted. A hundred times."

"My phone died!" Teddy protests. "Sorry, but... I met a girl at the party. We've been... Hanging out."

He looks bashful, but pleased.

"Christ," I mutter, overcome with relief. "All this, for a girl?"

"She's a pretty great girl." Teddy smiles again, looking like a proud kid. Because he is one. When I was his age, I was already deep in Barretti shit, doing my father's dirty work, but Teddy is fresh-faced and carefree, here on campus with nothing to worry about but keeping his grades up and partying with cute chicks.

*Because of Lily*, I realize. Because she's been sacrificing everything to keep him this way.

An innocent.

I think over the past few months, from the sleazy strip club in Vegas, to my brutal deal, and the FBI bullshit, too. All the fear, and anger, and pain she must have gone through—just to keep him safe. And she never said a word to him.

She faced me down—for him.

I feel a surge of protectiveness. I know I'm the one who used her brother as a bargaining chip, but that's all in the past now. She shouldn't have to bear the burden of his safety alone.

I'm here now. I can carry the load.

"So, nothing happened?" I interrogate him, just to be sure. "You haven't had any fights, any weird encounters with unfamiliar faces the past couple of weeks?" I turn to the roommate. "Nobody hanging around here who shouldn't be?"

The kid looks confused. "No."

"Why?" Teddy narrows his eyes. "What's been going on?"

"You know, I haven't seen this place since orientation," Lily pipes up. She links her arm through his and steers him to the door. "Why don't you give us the full tour? I want to see everything you've been doing. And hear about this new girlfriend of yours."

"She's not my girlfriend," Teddy says quickly. He follows Lily out, but not without shooting me another wary look.

Smart kid.

Lily pauses. "Coming?" she asks me.

I'm surprised. "Don't you want some time alone?"

She shakes her head. "I want you to get to know each other. If you want." She looks up at me from under her lashes, hopeful.

Damn. There's nothing in the world I could deny her when she's looking at me like that.

"Lead the way," I say, following them out. "But this tour better include lunch."

Teddy takes us around campus, pointing out the library, student lounge, and main hangout spots. Lily peppers him with curious questions about his classes and friends, but I'm content to hang back, watching them together. If it were any other man getting all of her attention, I'd be tempted to do something to stake my claim over her, but this is her brother.

The only family she has left.

Aside from me.

I feel a stab of guilt for my part in that, but I push it aside. The past is dead and buried now, what matters is our future.

Together.

Thank God it wasn't the Kovaks behind Teddy going AWOL—or anything connected to my dirty dealings. Lily would never have forgiven me for dragging her brother into my mess, and I wouldn't have either.

"... What about student theater?" Lily is asking. "You always loved helping out with the sets and lighting in high school."

"No," Teddy tells her, amused. "I loved hanging out with all the girls in drama club. Besides, I'm focused on film club. We're shooting our own short films next semester..."

I let them talk while I keep an eye on our surroundings, looking for anything suspect. I'm not a fool, and I know that despite our tentative arrangement, things could go sideways with the Kovaks at any time. Hell, they could go sideways with my own men, if they get wind of what I'm planning before I'm ready. There's still plenty of bad blood over Lily's dad turning on us, and the only reason Lily is safe is because I demand it. Teddy is a wildcard, but Lily never breathed a word about his location until this morning, so I'm betting he's safe here.

For now.

"This place has great sandwiches," Teddy says, nodding to a lunch spot with a line out the door.

"I'll go!" Lily says immediately.

"It's fine. I'll wait," I tell her, but she just gives me a look.

"You two get to know each other," she says, before taking off, leaving me with her brother.

"I didn't even tell her what I wanted," Teddy remarks.

I give a wry grin. "She'll know. I don't know how, but she can read minds sometimes."

"Right."

There's a long pause, as Teddy eyes me suspiciously again. "So, you two are back together, huh?"

I nod.

"And I'm guessing that big rock on her finger isn't an accident, either."

I hiss out a breath. "Nope."

Teddy's eyes go to Lily, standing in line. "We never talked

*Ruthless Games*

about it. Leaving New York. Everyone treated me like I was just a kid. Which I was, I guess. But I saw it. How scared my parents were, running. How Lily cried every night, trying not to let me hear. They never said his name, you know. Your father's. It was like he was Voldemort or something."

Fuck. So much for bonding.

"Listen—" I start, but he talks over me.

"My sister is the best person I know." He levels me with a look. "She deserves the world."

"We're in agreement on that."

"If she's with you, there must be a pretty good reason," he continues. "And I trust her on that. It's her life. But you should know something..."

He takes a step closer, squaring up to me. "If you hurt my sister, you'll pay." Teddy vows fiercely. "I don't know what your deal is, but she's been through enough. I won't stand by and watch her heart be broken as well."

I don't know whether to laugh or be impressed. I could kill him with one hand tied behind my back, but still, this wide-eyed teenager is showing more balls than half my crew back home.

I give him the respect of a serious answer. "I understand. And for your information, I have no intention of breaking her heart. I'll protect her. I promise."

Teddy relaxes slightly, but he doesn't get a chance to say anything else before Lily is back with our lunch.

"Roast beef, no mayo, hold the pickle," she says, giving Teddy his bag. "And you get the Italian," she tells me with a grin. "No complaints."

"I wouldn't dare," I say, glad just to see her smiling. Hell if I know how long it'll last, but after the stress of the past few hours, I'm relieved to see her happy again.

"Hey!" a guy calls to Teddy. "You still in for the lake?"

There's a whole group of them heading for the parking lot, with coolers and beach gear.

Teddy curses. "I forgot. But it's fine," he says quickly to Lily, "I'll go with them another time."

"No, don't be silly. Go." Lily gives him a grin I know is forced. "You should have fun with your friends. We probably need to be getting back, anyway."

Lily pulls him into another hug, holding on for a long time. I can tell that she doesn't really want to leave him, but there's not much a choice. He's an adult, even if he'll always be a kid in her mind and heart.

"Be safe," she tells him. "And for God's sake, keep your phone charged!"

She watches him bound off to meet his friends, and then turns to me. Her eyes are damp.

"Hey," I pull her into a hug. "He's fine. False alarm."

"I know." She hugs me. "But what if it hadn't been?"

I can't answer that. I don't want to. The danger of my world has always been a given to me. It was how I was raised.

But Lily and her brother... They're outsiders. They deserve better than this.

Which is all the more reason I need this truce with the Kovaks to work. Get out of the criminal game, and keep the Feds off my back, all in one fell swoop.

"C'mon," I tell her, guiding her away.

"Where are we going, back to New York?" she asks, looking tired.

I get an idea. I still feel a little bad for pulling that stunt in San Francisco, hijacking our day out to set up the meet. "I told my guys I'd be gone for the weekend; we don't have to be back so soon."

"You want to stay here?" she looks surprised.

"Maybe your brother and his friends had the right idea." I

smooth back her hair. "Let's go get lost—somewhere nobody will find us."

Lily smiles, and it makes my whole damn day. "That sounds perfect to me."

I drive us out of town a couple of hours, until there's nothing but fields and trees around. I turn off the highway, taking back roads until I reach a stretch of lakeshore, surrounded by trees. We walk through the woods until we reach the water, settling on a patch of grass by the edge of the lake.

I take a deep breath, finally relaxing. There's nobody for miles around, and I kept an eye on the rearview the whole journey here to check if we were being tailed.

We're completely alone.

I look at Lily. She's been quieter than usual for the whole drive, and I don't like it. I watch as she picks up small pebbles, tossing them in the water.

"You OK?" I ask.

"I don't know. This has been a hell of a day," she says, brushing her hair back out of her face.

"But it turned out OK in the end."

She nods slowly. "I can't believe I didn't think of it," she says, looking frustrated. "All this drama and worry because I thought something terrible had happened, instead of regular teenage fun."

"It's not your fault. I jumped to the same conclusion." I remind her.

"Still, I forget, he's just a kid."

"And I promise, he'll stay that way."

I can see in her eyes, that's what's really bothering her. That all my bullshit and darkness will somehow infect Teddy's life. Corrupt him.

"You can't promise me that." Lily looks away.

"I just did. Baby, look at me." I take her hand, and she turns towards me. "Nothing will happen to him. *Nothing*. I'll stake my life on it."

Her eyes widen. "Nero..."

"You're my wife." I say firmly. "He's your brother. That means he's family. You both are. And you know there's nothing I won't do for my family."

Lily reaches out and cups my cheek, her eyes burning into mine. "Thank you," she whispers. Then she presses her mouth to mine. Sweet. So fucking sweet I could drink from her mouth forever.

With a groan, I roll us, bracing myself above her in the grass as we kiss. Her body softens for me, molding to meet my shape, like she's made for me.

Because she was.

I'm hot for her, my erection pushing against the front of my pants, but as I trail my lips down her neck and across her chest that's exposed by her V-neck top, I'm not thinking about my desire.

I want this to be about her. I want to show Lily that she's mine. *Forever.*

I'm going to make it so good for her that she never leaves. Because as much as I like to pretend that I'm in complete control, I know that Lily will never be kept prisoner. If she wants out of this marriage, she'll go.

So I have to make her want to stay.

"Nero," she sighs in pleasure, as my hand slowly palms her breasts. She lifts her head, looking flushed. "Here?" she asks, looking around. "But we're—"

"All alone." I reassure her, peeling her shirt over her head. "Make all the noise you want, Princess. I know you like to scream."

She shivers under me, and I smile. Fuck, she gets so hot when I talk my filth to her, and I love to see it, every time.

"Nobody's here to see me working these juicy tits," I muse, my mouth capturing her nipple as I toss her bra aside. "Nobody's here to listen to you moan."

Lily's back arches as the bud hardens in my mouth. I use my hand to pinch the other between my thumb and forefinger, knowing just how much she likes that hint of pain.

She moans, her hips undulating beneath me, and I feel like there's fire in my veins, heating my blood. My erection is starting to throb, and it's so tempting to free it and bury myself inside of her slick warmth.

But it's more fun to watch her beg.

"Lift your hips, baby," I urge her. She does it eagerly, helping me peel off her jeans, and then her panties. "Let me get a good look at you. Fuck," I breathe, spreading her legs with my palms to reveal her swollen nub and glistening cunt. "Is that all for me? So pretty and wet."

Lily wriggles under my hands, her flush spreading to her bare chest. God, she's beautiful like this. Laid out on the grass with her golden hair spread like a halo. Pale skin glowing. Eyes on me, lip worried between her teeth.

"All for you," she echoes, an excited glint in her eyes. "What are you going to do with me?"

I chuckle darkly, power like a drug in my veins. "I've got a couple of ideas..."

I hook her legs over my shoulders, settling between them and slowly kissing my way up the inside of one leg. My lips brushing against the sensitive skin of her thigh.

Lily gasps.

"More?" I tease, using my hands to lift her ass, bringing her closer. Flicking my tongue just inches from her pussy.

"Yes!" she yelps, bucking to meet my mouth. "More."

"What's the magic word?" I sink my teeth into her thigh and nibble.

She half-laughs, half-moans. "Now?"

I smile too, loving the relaxed vibe of the water, and the breeze around us. It couldn't be farther from the buzz of the city. It feels like nothing else exists.

We're the only two people in the world.

And one of us is about to come her brains out.

My eyes flick up to meet hers as I finally reach her core, my mouth latching onto her. She's slick and hot, and I don't go easy. My tongue delves into her entrance, and her thighs squeeze around my head.

"Oh my god!" Lily arches off the ground, gasping. "Oh my god. Right *there*."

She tastes like heaven. I take my time devouring her, my tongue exploring her folds, easily finding her swollen clit. I swirl my tongue around the nub and Lily's hands delve into my hair, holding on as her hips thrust upward against my face. "Don't stop!" she chants breathlessly, urging me on. "Please don't stop!"

I love it. She's taking exactly what she wants from me, and I'm more than happy to give it.

I ease two fingers inside of her and her throaty moan fills the air. I work her up by sucking on her clit and moving my fingers in and out. It doesn't take long to bring her to the brink. I can tell she's getting close as her heels dig into my back and her ab muscles contract.

"Oh, oh!" she clutches at the grass, trying to find something to hold onto.

I start to move faster, growling against her wet folds.

"Nero!"

My name falls from her lips in a desperate cry as I feel her contract around my fingers. She comes hard, back arching off the ground as her body goes stiff.

Damn. She's like a work of art, riding out the pleasure. I'm lightheaded just watching her body writhe. The pounding desire in my bloodstream reaches fever pitch. I can't hold back any longer.

I need to take her.

*Now.*

I yank my pants down, freeing my cock as I move up her body. I still have her legs slung over my shoulders, giving me total access to her clenching pussy. Hot, and tight, and ready for me.

Fuck.

I sink inside her with a ragged groan. Lily's tight—she always is—and she moans, wrapping herself around me so I'm surrounded, every last inch. I'm so deep in her like this, I almost can't take it.

But fuck, I will. Over and over again.

"Nero," she gasps, and damn, I never get tired of hearing my name on her lips.

All those years without her, all the other women, they never meant a thing.

It was always her.

*My Lily.*

I drive into her. I start off controlled and steady, but my girl doesn't want that. My baby likes it rough. She bucks against me, curving her other leg around my hips to pull me in closer.

"Nero, *please.*" She's whimpering, needy, and that makes me wild.

I start to thrust into her in a frenzy. Short, rough thrusts are met with moans of pleasure and Lily kicks her head back once again, stretching her long neck. Her breasts are bouncing, and I'm mesmerized.

God, she's beautiful.

It's not just the way she looks either. It's the desperation in her voice as she pleads for more, begs me to go harder. The wanton thrust of her body, matching me stroke for stroke.

I can feel the orgasm building up in my body, tension that gathers at the base of my spine. I slow, shifting my angle, determined to get her there too. I want to feel her coming with my cock inside her this time.

"Look at me," I command, and she does immediately. I can see the fire in her eyes, the passion that is reflected inside of my own body. But there's more.

She's looking at me like I'm her man, like our marriage is as real to her as it is to me.

Fuck.

"Come for me, baby," I urge her, reaching between us to rub at her tight bud. Her moans turn frenzied. "Give it all up. I want to feel that pussy go off."

Another rub and she's there, spasming around me, the sweetest fucking feeling in the world. Her core milks me, like she's demanding my climax, and fuck it, I give it to her, every drop, spurting inside her as the force of it rips through me.

*Mine.*

I'd never felt an instinct like it before she came back into my life: To protect her, to cherish her with my life. But panting in her arms, I know, there's no going back. It's my ring on her finger, my seed in her belly—and one day soon, a baby too.

We're in this together.

# Chapter 16

## *Lily*

I should have known it couldn't last.
We're laying there by the lake, tangled up in each other, like we're the only two people in the world, when Nero's phone buzzes.

"Ignore it," I whisper, snuggling closer to him. There's nothing but the sound of birdsong and water lapping against the shore. It's a magical escape and I want to stay here forever.

Nero does. But then it buzzes again. Again.

"I'm sorry, baby," he says, sitting up. "I've got to check in."

My heart sinks, watching him answer. I already know, it can't be good news.

Nothing in the real world is ever good news for us.

Sure enough, his face darkens. "What the fuck do you mean?" he demands to the person on the other end. He curses. "And you're sure about it? Yeah, I'm on my way."

He hangs up and yanks his jeans back on.

"What is it?" I ask, bracing myself. "The FBI?"

He gives a sharp nod, helping me to my feet. "We have guys... Connected there. Sometimes, they'll slip us some intel, for a price. Well, it turns out, the raid wasn't a lucky strike. They had information about the whole thing. And it didn't come from the Kovaks." Nero scowls, his fury radiating.

"I have a mole in the Barretti organization. Someone sold me out."

I gulp. "Are you sure?" I hurry to put on the rest of my clothes, then we walk back to the car. All romance and escape is forgotten now with the news.

This is serious shit.

"Maybe the intel is wrong," I suggest hopefully.

Nero shakes his head. "It was too clean, the raid. Nobody should have known about that shipment, and there they were, waiting. *Fuck.*"

He drags a hand through his hair, and I feel a shot of fear. Through all of this, Nero has seemed invincible, but now I'm seeing genuine worry in his eyes. An informant inside his organization could bring everything crashing to the ground. Send Nero to jail, or make him vulnerable to attack from some other direction.

"We'll figure it out," I reassure him. "Whatever happens, you'll handle this."

Nero gives me a wry smile. "Since when did you turn into my biggest cheerleader?"

I swallow. "Since I'm a Barretti, too."

And if Nero goes down, then so do I.

We head back to New York and go straight to the house. His team is waiting there for us: Chase, Miles, Kyle, Avery, Vance.

I can't help looking at each of them with new suspicion. Could one of them be the mole? Nero trusts them, but should he?

"We need to lock this shit down," Chase greets him, looking

furious. "Whoever the fuck is leaking... They're a dead man. We erase him, his family, everyone. Nobody narcs on the Barrettis and lives to tell the tale. At least, they shouldn't."

He shoots me a glare.

"What else did your FBI contact say?" Nero immediately shifts into leader-mode. All signs of his previous worry are gone, now he's a stone-cold figure. He stands by the fireplace, assessing his troops.

"Nothing much," Chase sighs. "The guy works in the mailroom, so he only picks up bits and pieces. But he heard a couple of agents saying this is their play. They're coming for us, and if they have a rat... We're all fucked."

He looks at me accusingly again. "Which makes me ask, why the hell is she here?"

"Because I said so." Nero's voice is steel.

But when I look around, I see just as much suspicion in everyone's gaze. And why wouldn't they doubt me? I met with the Feds. I'm the outsider here.

And Nero needs their loyalty, now more than ever.

So, as much as I want to be a part of this, I play it smart. I take a step back. "It's OK," I say. "I'll be here when you're done."

I go upstairs, leaving them to discuss the situation without me. I try to distract myself, taking a shower after the long day, and then dressing in comfy sweats. I go to my studio and try to focus on my application for the Newton School, but it seems like the least important thing in the world, with Nero's fate—and my freedom—hanging in the balance.

*What happens now?*

I sit in front of a half-finished canvas, my mind racing. If someone is snitching to the FBI, that means I'm in danger too. Lydia swore to bring me down with Nero, and she's a woman who keeps her promises.

So what can we do? I feel way out of my depth here. If one of Nero's trusted lieutenants has secretly turned against him, then who knows what they're saying—or how we can stop them?

The meeting lasts an hour. I hear the front door opening and closing, and then Nero's footsteps on the stairs. He enters my studio, and stands there in the doorway, looking stern.

"Well?" I ask, moving to slide my arms around him. "Do you have any idea who it is?"

He shakes his head.

"But you're not thinking it could be one of them, are you?" I ask.

"Who the hell knows?" Nero starts to pace. "I was hoping that someone would give something away. A twitch of the eye. A nervous hand tremor. Shit, I don't know. I wanted to be able to look into their eyes and know if they were innocent or guilty."

"I'm guessing that didn't work?"

Nero shakes his head. "How do you spot a traitor? I can't trust anyone right now. I don't want to believe that any of them are the mole, but I can't be sure. It could be some low-level guy with a grudge. Or someone just looking for a payday. Hell, it could even be someone lured by the Kovaks to sell me out. I just don't know."

I try to think clearly.

"We need a list of suspects, and then a plan to narrow it down," I say. "Who had a chance to know about the shipment that got busted? You can start there."

"And then what?"

"Then... We set a trap," I realize suddenly. "If this guy is feeding information to the FBI, then give them something to feed."

Nero frowns. "I don't get it. The last thing we need is another leak."

I shake my head. "It won't be real information, it'll be bait. You pretend you're setting up another shipment." My idea takes shape. "The last one got busted, so you need to make up for that. You tell everyone it's last minute, top-secret, whatever. But you tell every suspect a different time or place for it," I add.

He breaks into a smile. "So they run along and pass that info straight to the Feds."

"Exactly." I agree. "You say you'll be there, too, to make sure everything goes smoothly since everything went to hell last time. The FBI won't be able to resist busting you in person, so they'll go all in with another raid."

"And we'll be able to see who the fuck leaked the info, depending on where they show up."

"Exactly." I smile.

Nero looks at me, impressed. "It's a good plan." He moves closer and pulls me into a kiss. "Maybe you've got a future as a criminal mastermind."

"No thank you. I just want to make sure we're safe," I say, cupping his cheek. "So this deal with the Kovaks can go through, and we can finally be safe."

"I want that too, baby," Nero murmurs. "So bad."

He kisses me again, before reluctantly pulling away. "There is one thing, though," he pauses.

"What?"

"You'll need to plant the info with Avery."

My eyes widen in surprise. "Do you think it could be her?"

"I don't know what to think," Nero replies. "But we have to include her as a suspect. I'll handle the others, but I'm worried that Avery will see right through me. She knows me too well."

I nod, nervous. "OK."

Then I pause, struck by a sudden thought. "You know it's not me, right?"

I search his face, needing to see it there. Needing to know he believes me.

Nero holds my gaze. "I know." His voice is gruff, but sure. "I trust you."

I exhale, filled with relief. "I trust you too," I whisper softly. "I don't want there to be any more secrets between us. Promise me?"

He hesitates for a moment. "Promise," he says, and then he's kissing me again, and nothing else matters.

It feels like we're in this together.

The next day, Nero figures out the details for the plan, and gives me the info to pass to Avery. I head to the club, my nerves growing. She's so tough and intimidating, I just hope that I can pull this off.

I can feel eyes on me as I walk across the bar, taking a seat on a stool next to Avery. It's a slow night, and she's going over what looks like financial paperwork while sipping on a Diet Coke.

"You're not drinking?" I ask, greeting her. "And there I was hoping for someone to go crazy on margaritas with me."

Avery gives a wry grin. "I only drink with people I can trust with my life... And that's a pretty short list."

"Huh. Smart. Good thing I'm feeling dumb enough for the both of us." I gesture the bartender over and order. "And keep them coming."

Avery looks curious. "Everything OK?"

"You mean, besides my husband ignoring me?" I make my

voice bitter. "He hasn't spoken to me since we got back, he's been too busy."

"Well... Things are pretty stressful right now," Avery offers. "Everybody's tense."

"Right. The mole." I roll my eyes, exaggerated.

"It's a big deal." Avery pauses. "Does he have any idea who it could be yet?"

I don't want to be suspicious of Avery. She's the only person around here that treats me like a real person instead of an enemy. She could even be a friend. But I can't help wondering if she's trying to get information out of me.

I shrug. "Not yet. Which just makes what he's planning even more stupid. I mean, running another shipment in when we don't know who's informing? It's crazy!"

Avery blinks. "I thought he was cooling it with that side of the operation, laying low."

"Nope." The bartender brings my drink, and I take a big gulp. "My genius husband thinks he has to step things up. That's why he'll be there, personally overseeing it. I made reservations for us Friday, but instead of eating filet mignon with me at eight, he'll be in some godforsaken warehouse on Granger Street making sure everything goes smoothly." I pout.

OK, maybe I'm pushing the 'spoiled princess' routine, but it gets the information across. Suddenly, I slap my hand over my mouth.

"Oh no," I cringe, hoping that I'm putting on a convincing show for her. "I probably shouldn't have said anything."

"Don't worry," Avery says, glancing around to make sure no one is close enough to overhear. "I won't tell anyone."

I sincerely hope that's true.

"Nero knows what he's doing," Avery assures me. I don't see any sign that she's planning to betray him, but I have to stick to this lie, just to be sure.

"I don't know how you guys do it. How do you live with the uncertainty of danger?"

"It's not easy sometimes," Avery admits. I sip my drink as she talks. "But Nero is a great leader. He cares about us, you know? Don't get me wrong, he's got that whole tough-guy thing going on, but he actually gives a damn. It's much better than when his dad was in charge. If I ever got popped by the cops, I know that he's got my back, just like I've got his."

The guilt from lying to Avery is almost too much, so I finish off my drink quickly and head into the back of the club, and down the hallway.

Nero is in his office, working. Stopping in the doorway, I knock on the open door.

"Hey," he says, leaning back in his chair. There are dark circles under his eyes, and I know that he didn't sleep well last night. This whole thing has stressed him out.

"Everything OK?" he silently looks for confirmation of our plan.

I nod, then carefully close the door behind me. "I did it. You?"

He nods. "Yup. I guess we'll see what happens next."

I round the desk. "I don't know how you do it, all this lying. The secrets. It makes my stomach hurt. Or maybe that's just the margarita. I drank it kind of fast."

He smiles, pulling me closer. "You never could hold your liquor. Remember when you got drunk on peach schnapps from your father's bar?"

I groan. "I was so sick. I can't believe I vomited all over your shoes. I thought you'd never call me again."

Nero smirks. "It was cute."

"My vomit was cute?" I ask, perching on his lap.

"No. But when you took off that private school blouse to clean up..." Nero's hands slide around my waist. "Fuck, I must have jacked my dick raw thinking about that white lace bra of yours."

I shiver. "Want to guess what color I'm wearing right now?" I coo.

Nero's eyes go dark. "What do I get if I'm right?"

I pretend to think about it. "You get to fuck me over your desk."

He stands suddenly, setting me down. "No bet, baby."

I feel a rush of disappointment, but then he smiles. "Because I'm fucking you here either way."

He reaches out, and suddenly yanks my blouse open, buttons flying. I gasp.

"Pink, hmm?" his eyes run over my breasts, encased in delicate pink silk.

"You like it?" I shiver, my nipples already getting tight with anticipation.

He grips my hips and lifts me, setting me on the desk, and wrapping my legs around his waist. "Yeah, I like it," he growls, bending his head to suck loudly through the silk. "Prettiest tits around, baby. All wrapped up nice for me."

He bucks against me deliberately, his erection pressing through his jeans and rubbing between my legs. I moan, heat flooding me.

"Shhh," he warns me, lifting his head. "Don't make a sound."

I can't help but whimper again as he rocks up against my core.

"I mean it, baby," Nero growls. "Whatever happens... Not one fucking sound."

Suddenly, he lifts me, spinning me around and shoving me facedown over the desk. I gasp, hands flat on the glass tabletop, hearing his buckle snap.

"Nobody can know," he commands from behind me, lifting

up my skirt and yanking my panties down. He lands a swift slap on my bare ass, making me jolt as he parts my thighs wider. "My guys need to think I'm working hard on this mole problem. They can't know I'm sinking balls-deep into the sweetest pussy in town."

Nero positions his cock at my entrance and thrusts inside.

*Fuck.* I bite back a cry of pleasure, but it's impossible to stay silent when he withdraws, and thrusts again.

Deeper.

So deep.

*Fuck.*

Nero bends over me, caging me in place. "You feel that, baby?" he demands, pistoning into me, grinding up high inside.

I whimper softly, spread wide for him. Cheek against the cool glass, but my body going up in flames. His hands rove over me, squeezing, gripping, taking possession in the way he does best.

"Please," I gasp, grinding back onto his cock. "*More!*"

"Naughty girl, what did I tell you?" He slaps a hand over my mouth, muffling my cries as he gets to work, rutting into me from behind. "Those moans are all for me."

But I can't help it, it feels too good. Nero's cock is surging inside me, owning me, hitting my sweet spot and making me moan and curse aloud. He sends my body jolting on the desk with every thick thrust, driving me wild. He's even more demanding than usual, like he's pouring his own frustrations into every thrust.

I can't get enough.

"Goddamn, you take it so well," he's groaning above me, hips snapping hard. He reaches beneath me, fingers finding my slick nub, rubbing it in a swift pace that makes me cry out into his palm. I'm trapped here, pleasure being visited on me at every angle, and God, I can't take it.

"Fuck, baby, I'm not going to last—" the groan he sounds fills me with excitement. Knowing I'm doing this to him.

Knowing I'm the one making him beg.

I can't hold back. Another deep thrust, and I shatter, clenching around him, my scream muffled by the weight of his hand. Nero's curses are lost in my hair as he pumps once, twice more, and climaxes, shuddering into me in a rush of heat. I spasm, my pleasure washing over me in waves as I hold him tight.

Because damn. Even with the walls closing in, and more danger surrounding us than ever before, I'll take it, just to be together.

There's nothing that feels as good as this.

# Chapter 17

## *Lily*

The days pass slowly, counting down to our big trap. Nero is stressed as hell, and I find it hard to concentrate on anything either, with everything hanging over our heads.

Soon, we'll know who's betraying him—and if we can keep the Feds at bay.

But still, despite all the drama and anxiety, I'm feeling closer to Nero than ever. He's not shutting me out anymore. This was my plan, and we've been over it dozens of times together, speculating over the suspects and who might be our mole. I finally feel like his partner, that he values my opinion.

I can only hope the plan is enough to reveal the truth.

Finally, it's Friday night. We wait at the house together, watching the clock tick closer to eight. That's the time we told everyone the new meeting was going down—giving everyone a different location.

Nero paces, wound tight.

"We'll know soon enough," I tell him. I'm fussing in the kitchen, trying to distract myself by making us dinner. I never cook, but tonight I figured I'd bring out my trusted roast chicken recipe, to keep my hands busy while we eye Nero's phone, waiting on the kitchen table.

"Here, taste this." I offer him a spoon of the sauce, but he just shakes his head.

"Why don't you try taking a few deep breaths?" I suggest, trying to calm him down. "This'll all be over soon."

"Will it?" he demands, running his hand through his hair. "Or will there be another traitor to take their place. Fuck, these days it seems like all I do is try to clean up bullshit, I'm sick of looking over my shoulder all day long. Whoever this is... They're going to pay."

I feel a shiver of unease. We haven't talked about what will happen when he has the name. He hasn't said anything, and I don't want to know.

Because judging by the look in his eyes, it won't be pretty.

"If this mole fucks things up for me... For this truce with the Kovaks," he continues, face set. "There'll be hell to pay. You know my whole family has been wrapped up in this for a hundred years? None of us had a choice, it was just what the Barrettis did. Family. Honor. Loyalty. Do you know how often my father drilled those things into me?"

He exhales, shaking his head. "I'm done. I'm taking this organization legit. And not one person is going to stop me. They'll be fucking sorry they tried."

I gulp. This side of Nero always scares me: The one who sees things in black and white. Ready for retribution.

"It'll be OK," is all I can offer.

He gives a sharp nod, eyeing the clock. Eight.

"Now, it's game time."

We wait. Suddenly, his phone buzzes to life. Nero snatches it up.

"What?" he demands. He pauses, frowning. "Yeah, give me a second, Chase is on the other line."

He stabs the handset, moving into the next room to talk. I try to overhear, but I can't make out much. After a few minutes, he returns.

"No die. There was no raid."

"What?" I blink. "I don't understand."

"Me either." Nero says, looking frustrated. "Everyone checked in, wanting to know where I was. Why I didn't show at the meeting spots. But no sign of the Feds."

"Does that mean none of the suspects are the mole?" I ask, feeling relieved, about Avery at least.

"Maybe," Nero replies. "Maybe not. Fuck, they could have guessed it was a trap, and decided to lay low. Who knows? I'm still just as much in the dark as before."

He scowls... Just as the smoke alarm goes off.

"Dammit!" I yelp, diving for the oven. "I forgot all about the chicken."

I pull it out: The roasting pan is blackened and burned. "So much for a distraction," I say, rueful.

Nero cracks a smile. "C'mon, let's go to dinner."

"Are you sure?" I ask, surprised. "Don't you need to work?"

He shakes his head. "What I need right now is to see my girl all dressed up, wine and dine her, and fuck all the stress away."

"In any particular order?" I tease, relaxing.

He gives me a wicked look. "Go get ready. I'm taking you out. And no panties." He slides his hands over my ass. "I want you wet and ready for me, whenever I choose."

We have dinner at a cute bistro nearby, then go for drinks at the new hot club in town. It's a million miles away from the vibe at

Nero's place, this one has a line around the block, and some trendy DJ playing loud music to the fashionable crowd. It's not what I figured to be Nero's scene, but I can tell, he wants a distraction, and I'm happy to play along.

We squeeze in by the bar, and get overpriced cocktails, Nero's hand resting possessively on my back. I like it. Being out in the world with him, like we're just a normal couple. Ignoring reality for a few precious moments.

I find myself hoping this is what our lives can be like, after the mole is revealed, and this deal with the Kovaks goes through. Not the trendy club, but the rest of it: Me and him having date nights, talking and laughing for hours, flirting and trading dirty talk before we go home and fall into bed together.

No more shady Mafia dealings or Feds on our tail. Just me and him, and maybe even a family, too, one day...

"You know I'm a lightweight," I warn him, smiling, when the bartender brings a massive fruity drink for me.

"I'll take care of you," he says, his hand drifting down to my ass. He squeezes subtly, and I wonder just what he's got in mind to *take care* of me. His hand searches, skimming lightly over my skintight dress. I dressed up for him, like he wanted: black bandage dress, with heels and a push-up bra.

"Good girl," he adds, throaty, and I smile.

*No panties.*

"I can follow instructions, you know." I reach up, to murmur in his ear.

"Damn right you can." Nero's eyes are hot on mine. He brings me closer, so I'm crushed against his body, the two of us in the crowd. "Maybe I'll tell you to get on your knees later," he growls, breath hot on my cheek. "Order you to open that sweet mouth and suck me off real good."

*Damn.*

Heat rushes through me. I squeeze my thighs together.

God, I love it when he talks like this. Nothing makes me hotter—especially now we're in a crowded bar, surrounded by people. It feels dirty, illicit.

And oh so sexy.

"Then what?" I ask, breathless. "What will you tell me to do next?"

Nero's grip on me tightens, and I feel his thick erection jut against my stomach. "Then I want you to strip," he growls in my ear. "Give me a nice long lap dance, like those girls up on stage." He nods to where some of the dancers are gyrating up on a platform. "Let me see what that beautiful body of yours can do. Show it off for me, get my cock good and ready for you."

I shiver in anticipation. "I don't think it needs any help," I tease, rubbing up against his thick ridge.

Nero groans in my ear. "Look at you, making me pop wood in public." He grips my waist harder. "Such a sexy little thing. I can't wait to get you bouncing on it, fill you up and watch you play. You make the sweetest sounds when you're coming all over my cock."

I'm halfway there already at the thought of it. "Let's go," I say, breathless and flushed. I couldn't care less about the bar or our drinks, not with the damp heat inside me curling, hungry for every filthy promise to be made real. "Let's go *now*."

But he pulls back, smirking. Lightly pats my ass. "No baby. I think we'll stay for another drink." Nero winks. "I love watching you get all wet and aching for me. See how long you can stand to squirm."

*Dammit.*

I give him a pout. "We'll see about that," I say, taking the cherry from my cocktail and slowly swirling my tongue around it. I give him a seductive look. "You're not the only one who can squirm."

Nero throws back his head and laughs. But then he sees something behind me, and just as fast, his good humor fades.

I turn, bracing myself for bad news—or the Feds. But instead, it's that imposing man from the ballet. Sebastian Wolfe. He's making his way through the crowd, strolling like a VIP with a gorgeous woman on each arm.

"Barretti," he says, greeting Nero in his crisp English accent. "And I believe this is your beautiful new bride. Congratulations. And to you," he adds, giving me a smirk. "Best of luck."

Nero scowls. "I thought you went back to where you came from."

Sebastian gives a careless shrug. He's wearing a designer suit, dark hair falling over ice blue eyes, and everything about him screams sophistication. He couldn't be more different to Nero's brutal, rough demeanor, except the two of them both carry the same aura of danger.

They're men not to be fucked with.

"I got bored," Sebastian replies. "Besides, I heard you were in a little hot water. Seems like you're getting a taste of your own medicine. I was curious to see how you'd fare."

"Just fine," Nero answers gruffly. "As you can see."

"In that case, why don't you stop by one of my card games sometime?" Sebastian asks. "It's a pricy buy-in, but I'm sure a man with your *resources* can find a way."

"Gamble with liars and cheats? I don't think so." Nero shoots back.

Sebastian looks amused. "Now, that's a case of the pot calling the kettle black, as my mother would say. Consider it an open invitation, if you can take the heat." With another smirk in my direction, he saunters off.

"I don't like that guy," I say, scowling after him.

"You and me, both." Nero says. He looks around, restless.

"You know what? It's time to bail. I need to get you home and naked."

"And on my knees," I remind him, flirty. He smiles again.

"Oh, I remember, baby. Hold tight, I'll be right back." He heads off towards the restrooms in back, and I sip my drink, waiting. Maybe one day Nero will open up and tell me about his history with Sebastian Wolfe—because clearly, there's bad blood there.

"Well, look at you, all dolled up."

It's Chase. I startle, almost losing my balance, before he steadies me, his hands lingering.

I pull away. "Is it two-for-one on assholes tonight?" I ask, smoothing my dress down.

"Huh?" Chase is gesturing for a beer.

"Never mind. What do you want?" I ask, already wary. "Nero will be back in a minute."

"Can't a man just have a casual drink?" Chase asks, a little too innocently to be believed.

"Well, you've got one," I say, as the bartender delivers it. "I'm leaving."

Chase grabs my arm and pulls me back. "You ought to play nice with me, Princess," he says, breath smelling like cheap booze. "You're going to need friends around this place... If you don't want to wind up like your mom."

He releases me, but I don't move. "What are you talking about?" I ask, my heart suddenly pounding at the mention of my mother.

I haven't seen her in eight years, since she walked out on my dad and Teddy and me. She went off to start a new life without us and didn't look back. So why the hell is Chase mentioning her now.

"Chase, tell me?" I demand.

He smirks. "Oh yeah, I forgot you didn't know."

He takes a long pull from his beer, taking his time. He's doing it to torment me, but I don't care.

"Know what?" I demand. "Chase, what the fuck are you trying to say?"

"That the bitch is dead."

I reel back. "No, you're wrong," I blurt, shaking my head. "She just left us, went into hiding on her own. She probably has a whole new family by now."

Chase laughs. "Jesus fucking Christ, you really believe that shit? The moment she bailed on you, she called up her old friends for help. We tracked her down easy. And we dealt with her, alright." He smirks, eyes boring into me, full of hate. "The way Barrettis always do. Left that bitch dead in a ditch somewhere, out in Arizona. Think they even chopped off her fingers, so they couldn't match the prints."

Nausea rolls through me.

Oh God, no.

*Mom.*

"I don't believe you," I whisper, even as tears prick in my eyes. "Nero would have told me. He never said..."

Chase laughs cruelly. "Yeah, I bet he didn't. The guy's cunt-struck, but this little nugget would have killed the mood, don't you think?"

"No." I shake my head again, searching desperately for an explanation that would make sense. "This was Roman," I protest. "Not Nero. He couldn't have known."

"Who do you think ordered the hit?" Chase retorts, his gaze shifting to Nero, who's making his way back towards us. "He wanted revenge on your family. He knew what he had to do—but he didn't stop there." Chase looks at me with triumph in his eyes as he drops the final bombshell. "He's the one who said to make it hurt."

My heart clenches, but Chase slips away before I can demand more information.

Nero rejoins me. "Ready to go?" he asks, smiling like nothing's wrong.

And all I can do is nod, a smile frozen on my face as I follow him to the exit.

My husband.

*The killer.*

## Chapter 18

### *Lily*

I stay silent during the ride back to the house. My head is spinning from what Chase said, but I can't process it. His words won't sink in, they just rerun in my brain over and over.

My mom is dead.

All this time, I thought she ran out on us. That she didn't care enough to stay in touch. It was devastating when she left, but over time, the hurt hardened into anger and abandonment, thinking she didn't want anything to do with Teddy and me. Like we weren't good enough for her shiny new life.

But all along, she was dead. Nero was the one who ordered it.

He has my mother's blood on his hands.

My heart is frozen like ice in my chest. I barely notice when we pull up at the house. I follow Nero inside, still numb.

"I think I'm going to take that lap-dance now," he says with a wolfish grin, closing the door behind us. He reaches for me, but I recoil in shock.

His gaze darkens. "What is it?"

I shake my head, backing away from him. "I... I... Can't."

"Lily?" Nero's voice softens with concern. "What's going on, baby? Talk to me."

He reaches for me again, but that just makes it worse. I wrench away with a sob.

"Don't touch me!"

My voice echoes in the foyer. Nero goes stock still.

"Chase told me." I blurt.

"Told you what?" Nero's voice turns guarded.

"What you did." I suck in a breath, forcing myself to say it out loud. "My mom's dead. You had her killed."

Nero doesn't say a word—but he doesn't have to. I can see the guilt written on his face, plain as day.

I feel sick.

"Oh my God, it's true. You..." I swallow hard. "You killed her."

I turn away from him, reeling. My world turning upside down.

"Lily..."

I whirl back. "How could you?" My voice breaks, and I hate it. "I've spent all these years thinking I'd been abandoned, cursing her name, praying she'd come back to us... And she was dead the whole time?"

Nero looks away. "It was Roman's call. He wanted your entire family to pay for what your father did."

The shutters are coming down in his expression. He's distancing himself from me like he has so many times before, but that's not going to make this blow over. He went too far.

"But you didn't stop it?" I demand.

"Why would I?"

I gasp. "Are you kidding me? Your father was in prison. He couldn't have hurt her. You didn't have to follow his orders!"

# Ruthless Games

Nero narrows his eyes. "They weren't just his orders. They were mine, too."

"No..." I sob.

"Yes," he growls. "Your dad knew what would happen, Princess, selling us out like that. Turning rat to save his own skin. He betrayed us, and that meant you all had to pay the price."

"No!" I cry again, but he doesn't stop. "That was the game!" Nero yells. "Don't you get it? You cross the Barrettis and you know what's coming. An eye for eye."

A life for a debt.

I can't take it. I flee up the stairs, sobbing, trying to escape the truth—about my mom, and the black depths of Nero's soul.

*How could he do this to me?*

I race to our room, and slam the door behind me, but a moment later, Nero throws it open and strides in. "You don't get to walk away from me," he growls, stalking closer.

"Yes, I do!" I spit. "It's over. I'll never forgive you for this!"

"So this is it?" he demands, looking furious. "This is your excuse to run?"

"My excuse?" I echo in disbelief. "My mom is dead. You had her killed! How can I ever trust you again?"

"Eight years ago!" Nero roars. "After your father ratted us out and nearly brought this whole organization down. After you broke my heart and disappeared! After she turned around and left you without a backwards glance."

I sob. "Stop it!"

I go to the wardrobe and pull out a case. Blindly throwing clothes in. I need to get away from him.

"See? You're running. Don't act like you haven't been looking for an excuse to go," Nero says, betrayal flashing in his eyes. "We said vows to one another! I swore to stick by you for the rest of my life, but you've had one foot out the door all along."

"Bullshit," I manage, but he gives a twisted laugh.

"Then why did you have divorce papers drawn up?"

I pause in shock. "How did you…?"

"Yeah, I knew all about that," he says bitterly. "I thought you'd come around, that you could love me. But it turns out, you never gave a damn about making this marriage work."

"Can you blame me?" I ask, my voice nearly hysterical. I'm not going to tell him I changed my mind, that I decided I wanted to be with him. That's erased now. "All you've done is lie to me," I yell. "All you've done is destroy my life! I could never love a man like you. Not when you have blood on your hands!"

Nero reels back like I struck him.

"You know what? If you want to go, then get out!" he yells, pointing to the door. "But you better be damn sure you know what you're doing when you leave, because God knows what happens next."

I inhale in a rush. "Are you threatening me?"

Hurt flashes on his face. "I don't have to," Nero bites out. "The minute you're no longer under my protection, there'll be a line around the block to get to you. What do you think I've been doing all this time, going crazy just to keep you safe? Those guards on the door aren't to keep you inside, they're to keep everyone else out!"

He strides closer, pointing. "The Feds will be the least of your problems. What do you think the Kovaks would do to send a message to me? Or even Roman's guys? Your mother wasn't enough to settle his score," he adds. "He won't rest until your entire family is wiped out."

I shiver. He's right, but I don't know what to do. I can't spend another night under the same roof as him.

I grab my bag and push past him. "I'd rather take my chances on them than you," I lie, hurrying back down the stairs.

Nero follows. "You aren't thinking straight." His voice twists with worry. "You can't leave!"

"You just told me to get out," I remind him.

"It's not safe." Nero scowls, blocking my path. I square up to him.

"And you're going to stop me?"

"If that's what it takes to keep you safe!" Nero roars. "Dammit, Lily. I will lock you in this goddamn house and throw away the key before I let anyone lay a hand on you. And you may hate me for the choices I've made, but I don't care," he adds, eyes glittering with fury. "If you hate me, it means you're alive to do it, and that's all that matters in the world right now!"

There's silence. He stares me down, like a block of steel. But before I can find the words to argue, there's a knock.

Nero turns. "Fuck off," he yells.

"No can do," the voice answers. "I have answers, on your mole."

Nero swears under his breath and moves around me to answer the door.

It's Vance.

"What's going on?" Nero demands.

Vance glances up at me for a moment before turning his attention to Nero.

"I've got a lead," he says. "My contacts got word, there's a meet going down. The mole and his handler, dockside off Porter Street, in an hour."

"How do you know this?" Nero scowls.

"I'll fill you in on the way. We need to get going."

Nero doesn't even look my way as he nods.

"You strapped?" Vance asks.

Nero pauses. "I'll get my gun."

He goes through to the office, where I know he keeps a safe. Vance stays in the foyer, watching me. He's Roman's man, I remember.

Was he the one who pulled the trigger on my mom?

I look away, chilled. Whatever's going down tonight, it's made him restless. He's got a fancy pen in one hand, and he's clicking the cap, over and over, like a nervous tic.

*Click-click.*

*Click-click.*

*Click-click.*

"Can you stop that?" I snap.

He narrows his eyes, and puts the pen away, just as Nero strides back out. "Let's go," he says harshly. He pauses in the doorway to look back at me. Our eyes meet, and I think he's going to say something, but he just turns to the guard on the door. "Nobody comes in except me."

The door slams shut behind them, and I'm left alone.

I sag back. I should be glad for the empty house. Getting away from Nero is what I wanted, but now I find myself anxious all over again about this meet of his.

But I shouldn't be. His safety is none of my concern.

Except…

There's something itching in the back of my mind. Something I can't quite put my finger on. Like song lyrics you go crazy trying to figure out, lurking just out of reach.

I shake it off and go back upstairs to finish packing. Nero's absence gives me the perfect opportunity to slip out. This time, there's no going back. I'll have to completely disappear.

And I'll have to get Teddy to do the same. He's still technically in witness protection, so maybe the FBI—

*Fuck.*

Everything screeches to a halt as the pieces slot together.

That damn clicking pen in Vance's hand that I can't get out of my head.

I've seen it before.

At the hotel, the one where the FBI dragged me for our meeting. I can see it so clearly: Lydia sliding it across the table to me. The same insignia in gold.

I sink down on the bed, my thoughts racing.

Because if Vance has that pen, if he's been at that hotel... It's too much to be a coincidence.

He's the mole. He has to be.

Which means Nero is heading straight into a trap.

# Chapter 19

## *Lily*

I don't know what to do.

If I'm right, and Vance is the mole, then he can't be trusted. This meeting he's taking Nero to has to be some kind of setup, a way for the Feds to finally get him connected in person to something shady.

The gun.

*Fuck.* He's walking into the situation armed. He'll end up behind bars again, and this time, I have a feeling that Lydia will find a way to make it stick.

Should I warn him?

I waver, my phone in my hand. A few minutes ago, I was sure that our marriage was over. My trust in Nero has been obliterated, after finding out that he's been hiding my mother's death all this time. Surely there's no coming back from that?

But still...

My heart aches. I dial his number. It goes straight to voicemail, like he's turned off his phone. Still, I leave a blurting message, telling him not to trust Vance, and to get the hell away from him. I hang up slowly, still on edge.

*What if he doesn't get the message in time?*

I look around, at my half-packed case, sitting on the floor in the house that Nero bought for us. *For me.* I should finish packing and run while I have the chance, but it feels like my head and my heart are at war inside me, keeping me frozen in place. No matter what my mind tells me, all the logic and reason in the world, my heart keeps sending me back to him.

I love him, despite all the betrayal.

*But is it enough?*

My gaze falls on a picture on the bureau, of Nero and me, back when I was just sixteen. A blurry Polaroid photo of the two of us, arms wrapped around each other, so in love, you can see it all the way through the frame.

Nero kept it.

For ten years, he kept that photo. Was he waiting for the day I'd come back to him? Because I was. All those years, deep down, I've been pining for the boy I'd loved with all my heart.

Longing to see the man he'd become.

And now I know him—too well. The darkness, as well as the bashful hope. His wrath, and his tenderness. It's all two sides of the same coin.

And I can't help but love them both.

His ring is on my finger. Our fates are connected, whether I like it or not.

We're bound together. Until the very end.

I grab the keys to Nero's car and slip out the back door. Kyle is out front, on duty, but I can't trust anyone right now. I hop the fence into the alley, and circle around to where Nero's car is parked out front. Kyle is watching something on his phone and doesn't even notice me until I'm inside the car and the engine starts.

"Hey!" he yells sprinting across the street, but I floor the gas, and peel right out of there, leaving him in my rearview mirror.

I can't stop for anything. I have to get to Nero, before it's too late.

I drive fast, my fear growing by the minute. I overheard Vance saying where the meeting is taking place, down by the docks, and I cut across the bridge to get there. It's nothing but warehouses in this poorly lit area, some abandoned and boarded up, and I slow to a crawl, eyes peeled in the darkness for any signs of Nero.

I reach the end of Porter Street and pull over. I can see Vance's car parked up ahead, so I climb out, wishing I'd changed out of my tight dress and heels. But there's no time for hesitation, every second could count, so I take a deep breath, and silently creep towards the building. I edge along the wall, staying in the shadows, until I can peer around the corner, searching desperately for any sign of Nero.

There!

I can see him, about thirty feet away. He's deep in conversation with some guy I don't recognize, as Vance loiters nearby.

There's no sign of the Feds, or any kind of trap.

I exhale in a rush. What if I got it all wrong?

But as I'm standing there, wondering what to do, I notice that Vance is ambling away from the pair, back towards the car.

*Shit.* Has he spotted me? I shrink back in the shadows, out of sight, as Vance glances around.

Then he pulls something from his jacket. He quickly crouches beside the car and fixes it beneath the driver's side, before straightening up, like nothing's happened. Then, just as subtly, he melts away in the darkness, like he was never there.

*What the hell?*

I'm still trying to process what I've just seen when Nero

finishes up the conversation. The other guy leaves, and Nero heads back towards the car, checking his phone.

He has no idea what Vance just did.

I open my mouth to yell a warning. Then I hesitate.

*An eye for an eye.*

That's what Nero told me, wasn't it? He was responsible for my mother's death. For all my heartache and pain. I could turn around right now and walk away, letting whatever happens just... Happen.

I could be free of Nero forever.

So why does that thought break my fucking heart?

Something snaps inside me. I have to stop him. I can't lose him like this. Not now.

"Nero!" I scream, running out of my hiding spot. But the noise from the river and passing traffic is too loud. He doesn't even look up. "Nero!"

I lunge towards him, desperate, when—

BOOM!

There's a blinding flash of light, and then a shockwave sends me flying, knocking me to the ground and stealing the breath from my lungs.

Oh God.

I roll over, clawing my way to my knees. There's smoke everywhere, flames billowing. I can't see him anywhere, there's no sign of life.

"NERO!" I scream, desperate.

But there's no reply.

I watch the fireball blaze, an inferno in the dark, and feel my heart rip in two.

Is the man I love dead?

TO BE CONTINUED...

Roxy Sloane

Lily and Nero's story comes to an explosive conclusion in Ruthless Vow - available now!

## RUTHLESS: BOOK THREE
## RUTHLESS VOW

I made a deal with the devil.

Mafia prince, Nero Barretti. The boy I once loved... And now the man who controls my fate.

I thought I knew the price I was paying, but he won't stop until I belong to him.

*Forever.*

Roxy Sloane is a USA Today bestselling author, with over 2 million books sold world-wide. She loves writing page-turning spicy romance full of captivatingly alpha heroes, sensual passion, and a sprinkle of glamor. She lives in Los Angeles, and enjoys shocking whoever looks at her laptop screen when she writes in local coffee shops.

\* \* \*

**To get free books, news and more sign up to my VIP list!**

www.roxysloane.com
roxy@roxysloane.com